EYES
OF *Stone*
TARA NINA

ELLORA'S CAVE
ROMANTICA PUBLISHING

What the critics are saying...

ဢ

4/5 Rating "Tara Nina's latest release, *Eyes of Stone*, is an intriguingly enchanting paranormal book. [...] The characters in this book are fascinating and quirky, with strong wills and intelligent personalities. Ms. Nina has fleshed them out wonderfully and has woven them into an edgy and complex plot. The story flows along nicely and Ms. Nina adds just the right touch of drama. I like how the passion and red hot sexual tension blends well within the story and doesn't seem out of place. This book is a fast-paced, page-turner that I really enjoyed. This is one that I will be adding to my keeper collection and one that I definitely recommend." ~ *Night Owl Romance Reviews*

An Ellora's Cave Romantica Publication

www.ellorascave.com

Eyes of Stone

ISBN 9781419958885
ALL RIGHTS RESERVED.
Eyes of Stone Copyright © 2009 Tara Nina
Edited by Briana St. James.
Photography and cover art by Les Byerley.

This book printed in the U.S.A. by Jasmine-Jade Enterprises, LLC.

Electronic book Publication January 2009
Trade paperback Publication February 2009

EYES OF STONE

&

Chapter One

℘

Bright lights flashed through the large front windows of Izzy's place of business, the Internet Pub. Sirens blared as the village's single fire engine raced past. Instantly, the pub emptied. Its patrons hurried to follow the engine and the throng of villagers that trailed behind it. Several were volunteer fireman. The others were curious onlookers who craved the excitement. Typical reaction for a small Scottish village tucked away in the Grampian Mountains. Left alone, Izzy watched the smoke rise in the distance as she stood in the open doorway. From the looks of it, she guessed the fire was located a few blocks over and near one of her father's rental cottages. She issued a silent prayer that no one was hurt.

After grabbing a fresh cup of coffee, she settled into the booth situated beside the center front window and stared out into the night. Whatever was burning made huge billows of smoke and flames shoot up into the sky for what seemed like miles. She looked up and down the street. It held the appearance of a ghost town. It seemed as if almost everyone in town must have gathered at the scene of the fire. In a town as small as theirs, people tended to pull together whenever there was a disaster. And a fire, well, that just seemed to be the most exciting to the locals.

She imagined the scene as she knew it to be from past experiences whenever a fire occurred anywhere in or near their village. People on bucket brigade passing filled buckets of water from one to another, helping the firemen douse the fire. Neighbors of the burning structure were probably out with their water hoses in hand, aimed at the flames. It was times like these, when neighbors pulled together to help each other, that reminded her of why living in a small Scottish village was better than city life.

Izzy sighed across the rim of her cup before taking a sip. This fire was sure to be the highlight of conversation for the next week. Oh boy. She couldn't wait. It was bound to be discussed to death. Sometimes, she missed the variety of topics that arose at the dorm. Local color wasn't as interesting as computer geeks, hyped up on coffee, pulling an all-night study session. Just thinking of her pals made her miss her days away at university. As she was slipping into a melancholy funk, headlights turned onto the main road.

Odd, it seemed to be coming from the direction of the fire. It being the only car on the road, she couldn't help but stare as it drove past under the street lamp in front of the pub's windows. She got a decent look at the passengers, which spiked her interest and had her straining to get a peek at the license plate. As she leaned back, it struck her that the woman and man she thought she saw in the back seat were just in the pub a day or so earlier. They were there the night one of the older computers had gotten broken.

Though she hadn't exactly seen what occurred, she knew how the one man ended up on the floor with the computer in pieces around him. Everyone in the place had told her varied versions of the fight. Amazing how each person saw the event differently. Izzy snorted, then took a sip of her coffee. Since the woman paid her cash as she escorted the incredible hunk she was with out the door, Izzy didn't bother to report the incident. Besides, the man who had been shoved to the floor was adamant that nothing be done.

That whole thing had added a smidgeon of excitement to her day. Not to mention it gained her enough money to replace an older computer with a top-of-the-line model, which should be here by the end of next week. Izzy smiled as she envisioned her new computer sitting on the empty table. Instantly, her fingers itched to set it up and be the first to try it out. She sighed. She loved technology.

Izzy stood, returned to the bar and refilled her coffee cup. On a normal night, she would be surfing the web right about now, in between waiting on her usual customers. Her place provided viable access to internet connectivity. In a mountain village such as this, it was an important service to the younger generation. Not to mention she sold the best ale, scones, tea and coffee in the area. Due to their location, internet connection was sparse and expensive for individual homes, making her place popular. Though she couldn't afford top-of-the-line computers for all sixteen of the stations she had set up, she tried her best to maintain quality access to the internet for her friends and patrons. At the moment she was down to fifteen computers, but with luck, the delivery of the new one wouldn't be delayed.

The fire had given the locals some excitement and ended her business for the night. She walked around the room, logging off the systems that were inadvertently forgotten by the sudden rush of people from the pub. She wiped down the seven wooden tabletops and slid the black vinyl chairs in underneath to make the place look neat. Then, she ran the cleaning cloth over each of the six stainless steel booth tables and made sure nothing was left on the red vinyl booth seats. Three of the booths were situated beside each of the three front windows. The other three booths lined the back wall across from the bar. Each booth and table held a computer station complete with a computer and an internet access connection. Three of the computers were situated on the bar, which ran the length of one wall of the pub. With the way she had the computers connected, her patrons could either use her equipment or connect their own laptops via the tabletop connection access box.

No matter how hard she tried, she couldn't pull her thoughts away from the fire, the car and its familiar passengers. This was the most eventful evening to have occurred for her in quite some time, other than the brief fight, which didn't count in her mind because she didn't actually see

11

it. She ticked off the ideas that sprang to life. If it were the pair that caused the fight in her pub, were they up to something?

Boredom got the better of her and she didn't bother to redirect her line of thought. It was more fun to imagine a diabolical scheme unfolding in her sleepy little village.

What were they after, if anything? She shook her head as the imaginary scheme unfolded, even though she knew it wasn't right. What if they were somehow involved with the fire? She thought she had just seen them in a car heading from the general direction of the fire. Circumstantial evidence, she decided. It wasn't reason enough to point a finger at them for maybe being involved with that fire. If it was even them that she saw. Izzy paced the length of the bar. The thick heels of her boots thudded on the tile, giving a rhythmic cadence to her thoughts.

With nothing better to do, she let the mystery fantasy unfold inside of her head.

What if there was something more underlying the actions of the couple against the other man that night in the pub? Her mind continued to whirl with possibilities. Was it a love triangle gone wrong or just a conflict between a prior lover and the new love interest? Izzy stopped pacing. Thinking back, Izzy didn't remember the woman as being beautiful. If her memory was right, the woman was more of a plain-Jane. Not much makeup, if any. What did she have that Izzy didn't that would make two good-looking guys fight over her?

Automatically, her gaze lifted to the mirror, which ran along the wall behind the bar. Being the sole owner of the pub, she dressed as she pleased. Granted, her style leaned toward that of a Goth girl with short spiky blonde hair, thick black eyeliner and dark red lipstick on her lips, which accentuated her pale flawless skin. Her clothes were the typical array of items worn by a Goth follower. Today's choice was a short black t-shirt with skull and crossbones on the front. Her bellybutton ring was a silver hoop with a tiny Celtic cross hanging on it and her skirt was a black leather mini. In her teenage years, this choice of clothing style had been more of a shock factor for her father than an actual intended selection. Now she kind of liked the way people stared at her when she walked past. It also made guys leery about approaching her. She was too much woman for one man to handle. Izzy decided, proud of her individuality. Following the mold society set for a businesswoman was not her style. Being successful, a computer genius and helping the local kids connect to the internet was what mattered most. If men couldn't look past the over-the-top clothing style and attitude, then she could live without one.

The ring of the church bell, which was used to signal the village that the situation was under control, reminded her of what initialized her train of thought. The fire, the two people in the backseat of the car and an incident that occurred in her pub, were they somehow related? God, she had to stop watching crime dramas on TV. Izzy tried to redirect her overactive imagination to another topic, but failed. Being alone in the pub wasn't helping the situation. It allowed her time to waste and not work.

What if they weren't fighting over the woman, but something else?

But what? And did it have anything to do with the fire? Odd scenarios played in her head. A thought struck her as she stared at the chip in one of her black-polished fingernails.

Izzy spun on her heels and marched to the booth where they had sat. As a computer expert, it shouldn't be too hard for her to find out what they were all about. But as she slid into the seat, she remembered the woman brought her own laptop to access the internet. There wouldn't be a history of websites visited by them on one of her computer systems that she could follow.

"Damn," Izzy muttered as she laid her head back against the booth. "And here I thought I was so smart."

Closing her eyes, a split-second image of the driver of the car flashed behind her lids. If she didn't know any better, she'd bet it was her father's best friend, Ned, behind that wheel. Sitting upright, she slid out of the booth. And where did every man his age hang out? Grant's Tavern, where else? If they were young, they were in her place, the Internet Pub. The old geezers frequented her dad's place at the other end of the road.

Izzy decided to close early. The crowd was probably still at the fire, so she figured the possibility of anyone returning was slim. And besides, her imagination had conjured up a mystery that she considered to be more fun to investigate than sitting around the pub alone. After locking up, she briskly walked to the tavern. Not a soul was inside with the exception of Willy, one of her dad's bartenders. She sighed heavily as she walked in and closed the door behind her. Everyone was still out at that fire.

Her heels thudded on the solid wood floor. The echo seemed loud with no one seated at any of the tables or at the antique mahogany bar, which lined the back of the room. The family crest hung on the wall behind the bar. Large wooden handles graced the beer and ale taps in the center of the bar. Each handle was carved into a different creature. The bear was her favorite. It controlled the Guinness. The back wall was lined with four tiers of Scottish whiskeys and assorted liquors.

"Hey there, Izzy," Willy called out as she crossed the room. "You slow too, I see."

"Aye," Izzy replied as she sat on a stool at the end of the bar. "Must be some fire. Any idea what's burning?"

"Yeah, your dad's cottage over on Beacon Road."

"Anyone hurt?"

"Not that I know of. You want a drink?"

"Sure, give me a shot of Macallan."

Izzy turned around, leaned back with both elbows on the bar and stared out through the front window. Well, at least tonight wasn't a total bust. She took the glass that Willy handed her and swirled the liquid before she downed it.

The town had a fire that stirred up some excitement for them to talk about for the next few days. And she...she had a mystery to solve concerning a plain-Jane, her man and the possibility that Ned might have been driving them away from the scene of the fire. Even though she knew this fantasy was a long shot, it was more interesting than her normal day-to-day reality. Suspecting that the fire held everyone in awe, Izzy spun around to face Willy and placed the shot glass on the bar.

"Hit me again, Willy," Izzy stated as she slid from the stool, gathered the darts off the end of the bar and launched one at the corkboard. *Bull's eye!* She grinned as she stated. "The darts tourney still on for tomorrow night?"

"You know it." Willy set the refilled glass on the bar behind her. "You playing?"

"Maybe," Izzy replied as she tossed another dart, which stuck directly beside her first throw. Damn, she was good. But then again, she'd been playing since she was three and her dad let her hang out in the bar while he worked. In his opinion, it was the best way for him to keep an eye on her after the death of her mother.

"Feel like taking it easy on an old man," Willy teased as he threw a dart and it landed next to the two already on the board. For a man of eighty, his mind was still sharp and his lean body moved with the agility of someone half his age. But it was his faded, red hair laced with streaks of gray that Izzy liked most in his appearance.

Izzy laughed as she caught the teasing gaze in his bright blue eyes. "Who do you think you're kidding here? I know you won the last tourney."

Willy dug a wad of bills from his pocket, licked his forefinger and thumb, then stated with a grin. "Care to make this interesting, lassie."

An idea blossomed. What she needed was information, not money. If she could just find out a name, then the information highway was sure to provide her with some sort of interesting fact about plain-Jane or the man who was with her. Izzy covered Willy's hand holding his money.

"Put your money away. Let's say, if you win, I pay you five pounds. If I win, you answer any question I ask."

Willy's brows pursed as he stared at her. He wasn't known to be much of a gossip. Quite the opposite, he was rather tight-lipped. The one thing she did know was that he liked to gamble, and when she laid her money on the bar, she knew she had him from the look on his face.

"Let's say I go along with this." He licked his lips nervously, then stated. "If I don't like the question, do I still have to answer it?"

"Depends." Izzy cocked her head to the side as she asked. "Why don't we just give it a go and see what happens?"

Izzy threw first and hit the center dead on. But Willy's throw did just as well. They were a well-matched pair in the game. Only thing, Izzy noticed the slight tremor in his throwing hand during the first few tosses. Deciding to lean the odds her way, she let him win the first game. After that, he was more at ease. Dart for dart during the second game, Izzy kept it close, but pulled ahead with her last throw to win.

"Okay, first question," she said as she refilled their shot glasses. "Do you happen to know who Ned's working for now?"

Willy's face showed relief as he answered. "Everyone knows that, lass. He's working for the rich widow who bought Castle MacKinnon awhile back."

His reaction made Izzy curious. What was he afraid that she'd ask him? When she started to ask him another question, he cut her off.

"Nay, lass. I won't be answering anything that you haven't won the right to."

Needing his cooperation, Izzy let him win the next game, but kept the one after that close so he wouldn't get suspicious. When she won, she turned to face him.

"Okay. Do you know an auburn-haired woman who is new to town? She's kind of plain, wears glasses and reminds me of a librarian."

"I can not be sure, but Ned told me that the widow's niece came to visit. Maybe it's her. Not too many tourists come this far out. You know that."

Willy tossed the next dart, shushing any further questions. Making quick work of the game, Izzy won and asked another question.

"Have you seen a rather large Scotsman who is new to the area? I'd put him at over six feet tall with long, dark hair worn in a ponytail."

It was as if she'd drawn a shade over Willy's face. He went from being comfortable to stiff. She watched as his gaze shifted from her to the floor, to the board, then back to her.

"That be a question best suited for you to ask Angus." Without giving her a chance, Willy walked behind the bar and started restocking the glasses.

He wouldn't even look at her, let alone talk to her. What had she said? And what did her dad have to do with this? Izzy slid onto the stool, spun around and leaned back against the cool, hard wood of the ancient mahogany bar.

In the distance, she could hear the sad, lonely siren of the fire engine. What a night. She sighed. It went from the typical quiet village evening to a hub of mystery. At least she was no longer bored. How could she be with a load of burning questions blazing in her brain? Who was plain-Jane and her Scotsman? And more importantly, what did they have to do with her dad?

* * * * *

The stench of burned flesh and hair filled his nostrils. Every muscle ached as he fled the scene of the burning cottage. One leg dragged and his arm was immobile and useless. Escaping unseen had been difficult, but he managed. His plan had not included a fire or the release of his enemy from a prison of stone.

No. Instead, he had intended to rid the world of the filth of their clan and lay claim to what was rightfully his. He'd researched his theory of the local myth in detail. Seven brothers were turned to stone by a curse. The clues he'd studied had led him to this village and the haunted castle situated in the mountains. Once the castle and its inhabitants had served as protectors of this village. Now they protected it. A handful of idiot locals interfered with a plan that should not have failed. Should have considered the possibilities of misguided loyalties from the villagers and the chance that they'd interfere with his plans, he surmised. That was an oversight on his part that would not happen again.

But even the best strategy sometimes met with defeat. Agony filled his low growl at the sight of his nemesis leaving in the back of a car, instead of dead. The roar of the fire engine in the distance informed him he needed to run. He took one last glance at the disappearing taillights of the car and then slithered through the hedges and into a dark alley.

This was not over. Not by a long shot. He stumbled with each step, but refused to fall as he distanced himself from the hotbed of activity the burning cottage had caused. From the deserted look of the area around him, the entire village must have gathered for the fire. He snarled at the thought. Imbeciles. While they were rallying to help, he was leaving the scene, free and clear. With the fingers of one hand limp from a dislocated shoulder and the simplest of movements causing him severe pain, he managed to pick the lock of a car parked a few streets away from the fire. He crawled inside and lay still, hoping he wouldn't be found as he caught his breath. Hearing no one near, he began the tedious task of hot-wiring a car with the use of only one hand. After several failed attempts, he succeeded in stealing the car. Idiots. He laughed. The whole village seemed mesmerized by the burning of a simple cottage, making his escape easy.

All he needed now was time to heal and reconfigure his plan. Though this setback angered him, it wasn't the end of his war against the MacKinnon Clan. Oh no. It was only the beginning.

* * * * *

In the early morning hours, Izzy gave up waiting for her dad to return to the bar and went home. Too tired to climb the stairs to her bedroom, she snuggled on the couch and soon fell asleep.

Visions of a gorgeous man filled her dreams. Broad shoulders, strong arms and hands, chiseled good looks and a chest that was better than a goose down pillow to rest upon teased her sleeping senses. In her dreams, his body was hard and had her aching for his touch. But his eyes were colorless and held no emotion.

No matter how many times over the years that this dream recurred, his eyes never changed. They were always without color or emotion. His eyes reminded her of the solid orbs of a statue, round and plain with simple etched dots for pupils. It should have scared her, but it didn't. Instead, she wanted nothing more than to ease his emotionless state. Wasn't it her right to have her way with him, after all, this was her dream? Why did her hero not return her desires? Why did he not look at her or touch her in return?

As she reached out to caress his face, a smooth hardness met her palm. Grazing her skin across his cheek, she received no warmth. He ventured no movement in her direction. When she pressed her lips to his, her kiss was not returned. Was he that hard-hearted that her touch repulsed him into a frozen state of shock? God, she wished she knew.

The more she attempted to make him return her kiss by rubbing her lips against his unresponsive pair, the rougher the skin of her lips became. All she wanted was a kiss, his touch, anything but this cold, hard resistance. Just once, she wanted him to return her advances, to ravage her mouth the way she tried to do to his with no response. What was wrong with him? Why didn't he move?

Izzy tossed and turned until she rolled off the couch and hit the floor with a bang. Startled, she sat upright as remnants of her dream burned bright inside of her mind. What was wrong with this dream? Or was it just this man? He'd starred in her dreams a lot as of late and never once responded. Who was he? Try as she might, she couldn't put a name with the emotionless face. Was he someone she knew at university? Izzy leaned back against the couch. This bothered her that she couldn't remember having met this man.

Faces of her friends and acquaintances flipped through her thoughts as she rubbed the sleep from her eyes.

The guys she dated at university were both smart and good-looking. But they paled in comparison to him. She sighed heavily as the figure of her dream man commandeered her thoughts.

If she wasn't mistaken, he was the hero in her childhood dreams, the one who always saved her from the monster. Her eyebrows arched at the realization. How could that be? She focused on images of her past. It hit her that he had taken center stage in her teenage dreams and had lingered into her early adult years. Why had this stone god of a man played with her dreams? Where had he come from? And where had he gone while she was away at university? Though she tried, she didn't recall dreaming of him much, if at all, during that period when she didn't live at home.

Izzy shook her head and tried to gather her thoughts. Had she dreamed while she was away studying? She felt certain that she had, but not of him. Why not? And most importantly, why was he back tormenting her in her sleep now? She'd been home from university for almost eighteen months, and if she remembered right, he'd returned to her dreams around the same time.

Stiff and with a bruised bottom, Izzy got up off the floor and walked upstairs to her room. Flopping on the bed, she curled around her overly large pillow and wished it was her dream guy. Try as she might, she couldn't figure out what had triggered his sudden reappearance in her psyche.

She really shouldn't overanalyze this, she reprimanded herself as she snuggled deeper into the covers. One psych class wasn't enough to make one an expert on dreams.

If he was here in person and not some figment of her imagination, she knew she could heat him up and make him hers. Squeezing the pillow tight, she wished it was her dream stud instead of a body-length stuffed replacement.

Even as tired as she was, her fingers inched downward to nestle between her thighs. With her eyes closed, she envisioned her stone-faced hero as if he were real and lying beside her. These were his fingers, not hers, playing with her clit and toying with her slit. In every dream, this man was pure perfection, tall, well-muscled and with the face of a god. She hungered for the erotic sensations that only this man could give her. Dream man was her sexual master, the one who could and would lead her into the world of ultimate climax. Though she had orgasms before, the ones with him would be unlike anything she'd ever known. It would literally rock her world, or at least that's the vision her dreams led her to believe.

Oh, how she wished he was here. Thinking only of him, she slid her fingers in and out of her dripping wet heat, pretending it was his cock. And what a magnificent cock it was as pictured in her mind, long and hard, ready to give her pleasure. The head was thick and plump and she hungered to lick the droplets hovering at its tiny orifice. Her nipples hardened with the thought of his lips tugging and tasting them. The longing for this invisible lover rose with the frantic rhythm of her fingers.

Rolling onto her stomach, Izzy bit the pillow, stifling her scream as the orgasm washed over her. When her breathing slowed and her heart returned to its normal pace, Izzy relaxed. Though the urgent need was sated, she longed for something else. As she snuggled into her covers, a little voice inside her head whispered.

You know what you want and you know where to find it.

Izzy tried to ignore the inner whisperings. If she knew where this man was, she would have gone after him. Didn't her inner self know that?

On a heavy sigh, Izzy closed her eyes and nestled against her pillow as his colorless eyes filtered into her dreams, luring her into the cold arms of her imaginary lover. If only he were real...

Chapter Two

❧

The next morning, Izzy opened the kitchen window and the lingering scent of smoke filtered in on the breeze. That must have been some fire. She shook her head and turned from the window. The sound of water running in the upstairs bathroom told her that her dad was up. Being the healthy Scotsman that he was, he'd want his breakfast when he got downstairs. And she knew the best way to get anything out of him was through his stomach. When he came into the kitchen, she had his favorites spread on the table and his tea cup filled to the rim with a special morning blend.

"Good morning, Isabo," he said as he planted a kiss on her brow and took a seat at the table beside her.

Izzy cringed at the sound of her given name. She hated it. The antique name reminded her of an old woman and not the techno-hip, chic go-getter that she prided herself to be.

"Good morning, Dad," she replied. "Anything salvageable of the cottage?"

"Nay." He sipped his tea, then continued. "It burned to the ground. What's left isn't worth saving."

"I'm sorry to hear it." She picked at the food on her plate as she planned her questions, then asked. "Any idea what happened?"

"Lit candles started the fire. Since we found no body, the arse I rented the place to must've gone out and left them lit."

"Did he at least show up and help fight the fire?"

"Nay."

Izzy couldn't believe it. Had the cottage been rented to the man and woman she thought she saw last night in the backseat of the car? Was that why they were headed out of town? But Ned wouldn't help someone destroy her dad's property. They were lifelong friends. Not wanting to start a problem between her dad and Ned, Izzy chose not to mention the car ride to him. That was something she'd investigate herself.

But there was something else nagging at her conscience. Was the man she saw and the tenant one and the same? Was that why Willie told her to ask her dad? It made no sense to her why Willie would be secretive about it. Whenever one of the two rental cottages was occupied, it became common knowledge in the village.

What else did the locals have to talk about other than a newbie? As she swirled the coffee in her cup, she couldn't recall hearing of the man who rented the cottage on Beacon Road. Had he been there awhile and she just hadn't paid attention? Nay, she decided. A man as good-looking as that one she would have noticed, even if his actions were suspicious.

"Any idea what happened to him?" Izzy asked as she glanced across the rim of her cup at her dad. His salt-and-pepper hair was damp and neatly combed. Dark circles lined the underneath of his hazel eyes, but that was to be expected, since he'd been out fighting a fire until the wee hours of the morning. His size reminded her of a bear. Gruff on the outside, soft on the inside and protective of his only cub, her. A slight smile tugged her lips as the memory of calling him her papa bear filtered through her thoughts.

"For all I know, he hightailed it back to that monastery over in Oykel." Angus MacDonell shrugged as he spoke.

"He was a monk."

Izzy couldn't hide her astonishment as her jaw dropped open. If the tenant and the man in the car were one and the same, in her opinion, it was a sin for a man that good-looking to be a monk. Angus reached across the table and gently closed Izzy's mouth. Startled by the sudden contact, she sat upright and tried to regain her thoughts.

If the man she met was a monk, he sure didn't act like one the other night in the pub with that woman. He sat a bit too close to her and his hands were in places on her body that a man of the cloth wouldn't have ventured near. Not that she was watching or anything, it was just something she noticed. She coughed, trying to clear the sudden dryness in her throat that accompanied the realization that she'd been inadvertently observing the couple during their visit to her pub. It had to have been his looks that held her attention that night, she surmised. The pair had been rather cozy, from what she remembered.

"The man I rented the cottage to was a monk named Brother Leod. I thought you knew that," he stated as he stood, grabbed his empty plate and placed it in the sink.

"If you told me, it must have slipped my mind." She ran a hand through her flattened, usually spiked, short hair. This kind of put a damper on her libido a bit. If the man with plain-Jane was a monk, then they probably weren't lovers, and this wasn't a lover's triangle as she had thought.

But why did he hit the other man in her pub? If it wasn't over the woman, then what was it about? Monks weren't known for violence. And what was he doing leaving town last night during the time of the cottage fire? Why didn't he stay and help? Since candles were involved, was he planning to forgo his vows and woo the woman? Had things gotten out of hand during hot and heavy sex? Was that why they fled the scene? They didn't want to have to answer questions that might embarrass them? This scenario seemed probable to her. But what if the man with the woman wasn't the monk and the other man involved was? Why hit a monk? Lost to her musings, Izzy didn't hear her dad speak until he said her given name.

"Isabo."

Chin tilted, she met his gaze and caught the twinkle in his eye. He was the only one who still used her birth name. In her heart, she knew he just did it as his little jab at her in reply to her rebellious Goth style.

"I'm going to the burn site. We're starting the cleanup first thing."

"Okay, Dad, see you later."

Izzy settled back in her chair as she sipped her coffee. This added a definite twist to her mundane existence. University life had been filled with classes, studies, parties and friends. Life here in her hometown was dull. But not today. She had a mystery to solve, which might possibly lead to an arsonist. Since the two policemen stationed in their village were on the verge of retirement, she knew the investigation wouldn't go far if left up to them. So she decided not to leave it up to them.

A firestarter, nah, she didn't see plain-Jane's man as someone who liked to burn things down. In her opinion, he seemed more the type to start a fire in the bedroom with the right woman. The fire was probably an accident of uncontrolled passion. At least, that was her theory on the subject. One thing this morning's chat had gotten her was a name.

Though he didn't look like a Brother Leod to her, it was what her dad had called him. And as far as she was concerned, it was a place to start. With nothing better to do, she planned to clean the kitchen, shower and dress, then scoot over to the Internet Pub early and spend some time scouring the net for Mister Hunky Monk. She laughed at the comical title she'd given him as she turned to the sink and the dishes.

* * * * *

"How could that be possible?" Izzy huffed as she sat back in the booth and glanced at the clock. Time was running out.

The class field trip would be there soon and she would be tied up for the rest of the afternoon with them.

After several hours of research, she found no trace of Brother Leod on the internet. Very little information was available on the monastery in Oykel. What she did find pertained to some whacked-out individual named Hume MacGillivray, who wanted to start some sort of dark colony of monks. How could the vast knowledge of the internet fail her? Because they're monks, she taunted herself mentally. They don't believe in worldly possessions and what use would they have for a computer?

Izzy slid from the seat, stood and stretched. The only thing left for her to do was to find Ned and have a chat with him about his late night ride and the passengers in the backseat. Hopefully, he'd clear up her questions about his male passenger and determine if the man was this monk, Brother Leod, or not. Seeing the school bus pull to a stop in front of the pub let her know that it would have to wait. The children had arrived.

Led by her best friend, Nessia MacKay, the children totaled twelve in all and entered single file.

"Good morning, Izzy," Nessia said and added on a whisper as she gave her a hug. "Glad to see you dressed down for the kids. Thanks."

"I know the school faculty dress code is strict and you stuck your neck out for me to get this chance to help the children. I couldn't let you down," Izzy whispered back as she nervously smoothed the front of her knee-length, gray linen skirt and tugged at the cream-colored silk blouse that she wore tucked in. Missing was her usual studded dog collar around her neck, dark red lipstick and thick black eyeliner. Izzy felt naked and plain without it.

When she agreed to help Nessia out, she hadn't realized that it required a dress code or she wouldn't have done it. The school dress code didn't affect her friend. Nessia was always dressed neat, kept her long, black hair in a ponytail, used sparse amounts of makeup, not that her fair complexion needed it, and wore flats to keep from adding to her almost six foot height. Looking at the eager faces standing around her, Izzy was suddenly glad that she agreed to help. They looked hungry to learn about computers and she was just the cook to feed them the proper knowledge to explore the world.

Nessia laughed as she turned to face her class of fourth graders. "Class, this is my best friend, Miss MacDonell. She has graciously agreed to share her knowledge of computers with all of you. Since the school has a limited amount of computers available, she agreed to have us come here and learn."

Butterflies filled her stomach. There in front of her were minds to mold and hands to hold and lead forward into her world of computer genius. Today had taken a turn for the better, at least where her love of computers and children were concerned. As for the budding mystery, it would have to wait.

* * * * *

"Wasn't his intention to burn down the cottage when he went in there last night, Angus."

"That I know, my friend," Angus replied as they poked around through the remains of the cottage. "I held my suspicions about that monk from the moment I met him. But the color of his money outweighed my good sense."

"Aye, that it can," Ned stated.

"Are he and the lass all right?"

"You can say that they're better'n all right." Ned glanced around at the other men, who had gathered to help sift through the cottage remains, then edged closer to Angus and lowered his voice so no-one else could hear. "They's managed to break the curse. Saw him up and about this morning when I dropped off Margaret."

"Nay." Angus sputtered as he stopped working and stared at Ned.

"Aye." Ned replied as he nodded his head.

"How?"

"Can't say," Ned stated as he shrugged his shoulders.

After a long silence between the two, Angus spoke, keeping his voice low. "The time has come. We need to bring the society together again. Tonight. My tavern. Nine o'clock. See that the word is spread."

Ned nodded, then eased away from Angus as if nothing had conveyed between them.

This was news he had never expected to hear in his lifetime. A MacKinnon was free of the curse. But how? A meeting of the society was definitely in order. This news needed to be shared. Two hundred years the society had protected the secret of the MacKinnon clan. Seven brothers cursed. Seven brothers hidden and their whereabouts kept secret, protected from everyone...everyone except the society.

The only brother who wasn't under their jurisdiction was the one who was set free. Akira had hidden and protected that one. Why now was he released from the curse? What was at stake? And more importantly, where did that leave the other brothers?

Angus ran a shaky hand through his hair. After so much time, could they even find the brothers? And now that a way to break the curse had surfaced, could they set them free? Could he risk the others simply because one had found his freedom?

This was an event Angus never expected to have to face. It hadn't occurred to him that he would be the MacDonell male faced with such a difficult decision concerning the MacKinnon brothers' fate.

* * * * *

Izzy sat behind the bar at the Internet Pub and stared across the top of her laptop at the regulars who frequented her place. Tim McGee was a short, red-haired man who reminded her of a leprechaun. He was here every night, sat in the corner and surfed the internet uninterrupted for hours. Amy and Annie Fergusen were strawberry blonde-haired twins in their junior year of high school, who managed to do their homework assignments and research universities on the old computer beside one of the front windows. There were others who visited on a regular basis, but not like these three.

Then again, there was Colin Campbell.

She had known Colin all of her life. They played together as children, went to school together and spent so much time together, they were thought of as brother and sister. They fought like siblings and he protected her as if he were her older brother. He even called her every Sunday when she was away at the university. After graduation, it had been his idea to create a place where the people of Lochsbury and its neighboring villages could have internet access. It was the lure of providing a necessary escape for the young adults of her hometown that brought her back instead of taking a job with some software research firm in London. Besides, she liked being her own boss.

As if he were cued in to her thoughts, Colin walked through the door. He eased behind the bar and laid a friendly kiss to her cheek.

"How's things tonight?" He slurred slightly in his thick Scottish brogue and the scent of strong mead flowed on his words.

"Been nipping at your daddy's home brew, now haven't ya," Izzy jested.

"Aye, lassie." He wagged his bushy red eyebrows at her as he continued. "When your pappy asks you to try his latest batch, you can not be turning him down, now can you?"

"No, Colin. I'm smelling you couldn't," she teased as she waved her hand in front of her nose comically, clearing the stench of stale mead from the air. Colin made himself comfortable on a stool behind the bar beside her.

"Quiet bunch you got in here." He nodded toward her patrons.

Izzy nodded, then returned to scouring the internet for any information she could find on the monastery over in Oykel. If there was nothing on Brother Leod himself, then maybe she could find out something about the monastery. Odd tidbits concerning a fraternal order named the Brotherhood of Our Sons of the Servant of Judgment, seemed to be connected to the monks and a strange man named Hume MacGillivray. But so far, she hadn't been able to determine the relationship.

Just when she was about to quit, a dark-colored website popped up. It hinted at black magic and spells, witches and warlocks, or at least that's the tone she grasped from the site. Clicking through the pages, she found a registration form. Skimming through it, she was surprised to find a name she recognized. Brother Leod. It was the first mention of him anywhere. Was it the same man who rented her dad's cottage, burned it to the ground, then disappeared?

If she filled in this form, would it lure him into the open?

Was it worth a try? And what did it mean by no one without the true desire for diabolism need apply, and those with natural gifts and the ability for devout loyalty shall be rewarded? Who and what was this guy recruiting? And more importantly, who did he think he was?

This site had to be a joke. She almost clicked away, but at the last second didn't. What if this was their only clue to finding Brother Leod and a possible answer to the curse? This was the only lead she'd found. Was this or wasn't this the man they needed? Though he may or may not have the anti-curse that would save Ian, Izzy couldn't chance losing the opportunity. There was only one way to find out. Izzy filled out the form with vague information. If it turned out not to be the person she was looking for, then this strange group wouldn't be able to find her with the information she listed.

Colin poured two drinks, then leaned over her shoulder to peek at the screen.

"Hold on there, Izzy," he stated as he stopped her hand by placing the glass on the back of it. "What'cha fillin' out there?"

Izzy took the glass and set it on the bar beside her laptop. Without looking up at Colin, she continued to type. "I'm joining this little Brotherhood of Our Sons of the Servant of Judgment. It seems the monk that burned down my dad's cottage is recruiting new members. Maybe by joining, I can gain information on his location."

"I know you're not putting in your real information on that now, are you?" Colin questioned.

"Colin, I can't believe you asked that," she stated in a mock tone of disgust. "I'm smarter than that. I'm using that postal box I've got set up for the business and one of those freebie e-mail accounts I used in college as the contact. And I'm not even listing my real name on here. According to this, I'm Inez and my e-mail name is technonerd. I'm just using it as a ploy to gain information and find out if this is even the right Brother Leod."

"What if it isn't him? How do you get out of this brotherhood? Is there a fee to join?" Colin rambled on without giving her a chance to answer. "And what are you doing trying to catch this guy anyway?"

"It looks like no money changes hands. Everything on the site seems to talk in a circle, hinting at, but not actually claiming to be involved with black magic and some sort of Devil worship." Izzy stated in a nonchalant manner as she shrugged, hoping Colin wouldn't get involved. He had a tendency to get in her way when it came to things he deemed dangerous. And this, she felt certain, he'd proclaim as something she shouldn't do. She saved a copy of the form to a file in her documents, then sent it to the printer at the end of the bar.

She turned to face him as she continued in as innocent a tone as she could muster. "Besides, if I find anything, I'll turn it over to our trusted law enforcement officers, Stan and Merle. You know that, don't you?"

Without answering her, Colin retrieved the copy for her, but didn't hand it to her directly. He sat staring at the paper and mumbling.

"Brotherhood...sons...servant...judgment, where have I heard that before?"

While he mumbled, she claimed the paper from his hand. As if he'd suddenly become sober, his glassy green eyes widened and he sat upright. Izzy could tell that the wheels of thought were turning, but he didn't give her a chance to ask. Instead, he got off his stool, kissed her sloppily on the cheek and left with a simple, "Catch ya later, Izzy."

Now that was odd. Did he know something she didn't? Obviously, he did.

Chapter Three

ഔ

With each glance at the clock, its hands appeared to be frozen. Time dragged before the last of her three patrons finally left at half past nine p.m. Instead of waiting until the usual closing time of ten, she shut everything down and locked up.

Colin's strange behavior earlier had her mind whirling with questions and her fingers typing furiously on the keyboard. It turned out that the so called Brotherhood of Our Sons of the Servant of Judgment had been around for over two hundred years. From everything she'd read, it seemed to her that the creator of the brotherhood, Hume MacGillivray, had a strange vendetta against something or someone. But nowhere in her research did she find out exactly what they crusaded against, or for. Was she reading too much in the vague facts she found floating around on the internet?

No, she shrugged as she adjusted her grip on the laptop she had tucked under her arm. Something wasn't right with this Brother Leod and his odd little brotherhood and she planned to find out what. When she neared her dad's bar, she noticed the car from the night before that had contained the two mystery passengers in the backseat. It had to be Ned's. He had to be here.

As she pushed open the door to Grant's Tavern, she realized that she'd forgotten something. Tonight was the darts tourney. Nearly every man from the village and from miles around, old and young, had gathered to enter this event. The bar was crowded with men drinking, wagering and discussing their favorites to win.

Many of the faces she knew were from the village. Some were from neighboring towns and there were a few she couldn't place. But that didn't matter. What did was the fact that she couldn't find her dad or Ned. It wasn't like her dad to miss a tourney and Ned never skipped an opportunity to place a bet.

Making her way through the crowd, she returned each greeting politely and somehow managed to keep the conversations to a minimum until she finally reached the bar. Willie was manning the taps, while two other bartenders scurried around like trapped mice, taking orders and filling glasses. Tourney night always brought out a crowd. Not seeing her dad, she knew the best way to find him was to stay put.

"Looks like you could use some help," Izzy said to Willy as she eased behind the bar and slid her laptop into the safety of a cubby underneath the counter.

"You be a sight for sore eyes, lassie." Willie replied, then grinned.

"Where's Dad? Shouldn't he be here?"

Izzy noted the shift of his eyes to the office door, then back to her before he spoke.

"He had a meeting that couldn't wait. Should be done soon enough."

Now she knew something was definitely wrong. It wasn't like her dad to miss a tourney, especially one hosted by his own bar. He was known for being a master of ceremonies and made each tourney a grand event. No man left his bar without feeling welcomed, and a bit tipsy to boot. Being holed up in his office was not the normal.

Nope, this wasn't like him at all, Izzy surmised as she tied on her green apron. She smoothed out the wrinkles so the Grant's Tavern logo of an overflowing mug engraved with the Celtic cross was more visible and the apron fit more comfortably.

Without missing a beat, Izzy stepped into the role of waitress. It was a position she knew well. For years, she spent her afternoons, evenings and weekends at Grant's Tavern. After the death of her mother, her dad was all she had and the bar was their family business. To be near him, she hung out at the bar and learned to throw darts at an early age. With age, she learned to tend tables and bartend. Both were skills that helped pay the bills when she was away at the university.

The lure of computers and the vast world outside of Lochsbury made her hunger for a different pace. Boy, had that been a fight. She snorted as she gathered the empty glasses from the tables and loaded them onto her tray to take into the back room to clean. Her dad didn't like the idea of his only child off at some university far away. But in the end, he caved to her wishes as always, especially since her best friend, Nessia, was going with her.

Four years at the University of Strathclyde, in Glasgow, had been a much-needed escape. Not only did it give Izzy the freedom to explore the academic world, it gave her the chance to develop her sexual awareness. But that was something her dad didn't need to know. A wicked smile tugged at her lips at a memory of a particular dorm room dart game that took a new twist and became a game of strip darts. Of course, she won and it was her first experience of girl on girl action.

Oh, what an experience. She sighed as she placed the dirty glasses in the dishwasher. Just thinking of the night they drank a couple of bottles of wine and invented the game of strip darts made Izzy tingle in between her thighs. They were young and neither knew enough to fill a thimble about sex. Instinct stepped in and took over, guiding them into a thorough exploration of each other's bodies, which left them naked and sexually spent in each other's arms.

That was just the start. Together, they made strip darts a campus phenomenon. It spread from dorm to dorm and they were labeled as the inventors of a new tradition. Even though Izzy suspected that strip darts wasn't a new concept. It had probably been done somewhere already. Sexual freedom was grand during her time away, but it had always lacked something.

Izzy replaced the dirty glasses on her tray with clean ones. Leaning against the counter, she shook inwardly as the memories of heated sexual encounters within her circle of friends surfaced to the forefront of her thoughts. Every ounce of her hungered for the fantastic sensations the hands of a lover could bring. But no matter what she tried, there had been that little slice of heaven missing. That over-the-top orgasm she craved eluded her.

"Hey, Izzy, we need those glasses out front."

Willy's voice shot her into a taut upright stance, snapping her out of her thoughts. Heat crept to her cheeks as she laughed to herself. Man, if he could've read her thoughts. But he couldn't and she was thankful. Gathering the tray to her shoulder, Izzy stepped through the swinging door and back behind the bar.

After replacing the glasses under the bar, she worked her way around the crowd, taking drink orders and keeping an eye on the office door.

* * * * *

"You can not be serious, Angus," Timothy Mcfae stated on a huff. "A MacKinnon freed, not possible."

"Aye, that legend's over two hundred years old," Lonnie Grooms added. "A story repeated for children to be believing, not grown men."

"Enough of your grumbling," Angus snapped as he pounded a meaty fist on his desk. "You are all sworn members of the society. We are bound to protect the brothers. Whether you be believing or not, each of your ancestors took an oath and that oath lies within your hands to honor."

Angus stared at each man as a hush filled the room. For as long as he could remember, the descendents of six different clansmen were chosen to uphold the vows given to a lively woman named Akira. It was their sworn duty to hide and protect her cursed brothers from the evil that placed their souls within a solid form of stone. That was how the story went that was told from one head of the clan to another.

But much had been lost over the generations. Details vanished. Exact locations of where these statues were hidden had long been forgotten. All that remained were the vague memories handed down from one son to another.

This could be bad, Angus thought as he shook his head. Even he, as the leader of the society, didn't know where his ancestor had hidden the brother that he'd been given the duty and honor to protect. Bloody hell, he couldn't even be sure which of the MacKinnons his own clansman had hidden. And until now, he hadn't even been sure there was any fact to the tale.

Angus stood and glanced from face to face. Each man in the room had been a member of the society for as long, if not longer, than he. Over the years, the membership had grown. Instead of just one representative from each of the original six clansmen, there were two and sometimes three men from each clan gathered for these meetings. The premise of the society had turned more into a gentlemen's club than a brotherhood of protectors and Angus knew it was time to turn that around. Gone was the friendly nature of their occasional gatherings for drinks, games and tall tales. The society had a mission that must be upheld. It was up to him to reinstate that purpose and carry through with the promises of their ancestors. The MacKinnon brothers must be found.

"Gentlemen." Angus cleared his throat and continued. "The time has come that we must uphold the original manifest of this society. Our ancestors believed that the curse was real. Thus, we must believe in them."

"As I said earlier," he continued with his speech while he held their full undivided attention. "A MacKinnon has been freed. How? I can't say. But I speak the truth. Several of you have even seen him in me very own tavern."

Glancing around the room, he noted heads bobbing in acknowledgement. This looked promising with the exception of Lonnie and Timothy, who stood in the rear with their backs against the wall and their arms crossed over their chests. Young and rebellious to the old ways, Angus thought with a sigh. Those two would be trouble, without a doubt.

A subtle nod from Colin as he eased to the back of the room and Angus knew the situation would be diffused. That young man would make a decent politician. Angus snorted. But then Izzy wouldn't have anything to do with him. Rebellious by nature, his daughter wouldn't associate with a politician, even if he was her best friend.

"It is up to us to locate the brothers," Angus stated, returning his attention to the group. The roar of the crowd outside the door reminded him of the tournament and his responsibilities to the game. This meeting needed to come to an end before suspicions concerning his absence from the bar arose. "Our ancestors hid them. Now the time has come for us to find them. Consider it a scavenger hunt."

With those words said, he noted the sudden interest of the two young men in the rear, who earlier held no belief in the matter. Make it a game. Reward a prize and those two might actually help. Angus hated what sprang to life in his head, but he could think of no other route to guarantee full cooperation from the group. Without every descendant's help, the possibility of finding and freeing all of the brothers was fruitless. As it was, he wasn't even sure he could find the MacKinnon his family hid.

"What do we get if we find these so-called MacKinnon brother statues?" Lonnie questioned in a mocking tone.

"Your dignity," Ned quipped.

Colin stepped in front of Lonnie, preventing him from acting on the impulse to lunge at the older man. The attention a fight in the office would bring from the crowd in the bar was not a situation Angus wanted to deal with at the moment. The society and its actions were secret. It had to remain that way if they were to complete the obligations of their ancestors. Angus bit back his rising anger and decided to finish his thought on turning the hunt into a game with a reward at the end. If that was what it took to secure the help of all the society members, then that was how he'd handle it.

"For each member who locates and brings a MacKinnon brother's statue to this establishment, you will receive a handsome reward."

"How much," Timothy yelled.

Angus' jaw tightened as he stared at the two young men in the back. A quick glance about the room and he knew others showed an interest in the money. Could he blame them? He shook his head slightly. Most of the men came from neighboring villages and towns, where money was tight. On a heavy sigh, he spouted an amount, though it knotted his gut to think that he may have to part with his own hard earnings in order to uphold the vows of the society and his ancestors.

"Five thousand Euros per MacKinnon brother's statue."

Ned's hand landed on Angus' shoulder as the shorter man stood on a chair and added stipulations to the quest.

"Each statue must be a proven brother. One of the seven stated to be cursed. It was the eldest brother, Gavin, who was released. It's the other six that you must find. Each must be brought here in solid condition. You mustn't try to open the statues, for the curse is real. Good luck and God's speed."

Before Ned stepped off the chair, Timothy and Lonnie scooted out the office door. With the way they hurried out, it was obvious that they were in it for the money and not the honor of the deed. Angus shook his head as he stared at the open doorway. The elders of the society remained, as well as Colin.

"You think you should have told 'em about the evil which lurks in pursuit of said same statues," old man Thicket stated as he moved to stand behind Ned and Angus.

"Nay," Ned snickered. "Let 'em learn on their hotheaded own."

A ripple of nervous laughter cut through the thick tension in the room.

"You know we are all behind you on this, Angus," another of the elder members stated. "It's only right we live up to the oath given by our ancestors. Money or no, we shall see this through."

Each man shook his hand and gave their promise of help as they exited the room. These men he trusted. But the other two...he held his doubts.

* * * * *

Izzy bumped her hip into the corner of a table when Timothy and Lonnie shot out of the office, barreled through the crowd and pushed a patron into her back. If it wasn't for the man's quick reflexes, the tray of drinks she was carrying would have spilled.

"We can't have you wasting good ale, now can we?" The older gentleman quipped as he helped Izzy regain her balance.

"You're right. It would be a sure sin," Izzy grinned, trying to add humor to her voice, though she wanted to toss a mug at the back of Timothy McFae's exiting head.

What business that idiot and his counterpart, Lonnie, had with her father piqued her interest. Those two weren't known for their mental abilities or their trustworthiness. What did her father want with them that couldn't wait until after the darts tournament? After delivering the last of the drinks, she worked her way through the crowd toward the office door. One by one, she recognized each man that walked out and rejoined the crowd. These men were her father's friends. Over the years, she had seen them meet in the office, drink and gamble.

But from the looks of them, this meeting was different. Something wasn't right. When Colin walked out behind his father and wouldn't meet her gaze, she knew her hunch was right. This wasn't a normal meeting of the gentlemen's club, it was about something specific. Did it have to do with the mysterious Brother Leod and the burning of her father's cottage? Had Colin told her father about the website she found and joined? Was she right in thinking that the Brother Leod recruiting dubious individuals and the one who rented the cottage were the same?

And the question that nudged at her brain the most...what was behind this impromptu meeting of the gentlemen's club? Surely her father wouldn't plan it for the same night as a dart's tournament, not when he was the ringmaster of the event. No, there was definitely something wrong and she was determined to find out what.

Getting to her father was harder than she anticipated. He slipped out the door and was acting as the master of ceremonies within a matter of seconds. Was he avoiding her? Izzy was certain that he was.

The first chance she got, Izzy snuck into the office. A quick perusal gave her no clues as to what had taken place. No notes were lying about. No visible information caught her eye. As usual, his desk was not locked and nothing was out of place that her search could detect. As quietly as she had entered, Izzy slipped back out into the crowd.

This was going to be tougher than she thought. Looking up, she caught Colin's gaze for a split second before he averted his eyes.

Then again, she thought as a devious smile upturned her lips, there was one person she could pry for information.

Chapter Four

℘

It was after midnight before the last dart was finally thrown and the winner was announced. The party that followed kept the tavern open until two in the morning. Izzy's feet were sore and her back ached, but her mind buzzed with questions. Pinning her father down was another problem. Sometime during the last hour, he slipped away, leaving her and the others to clean up and close.

That was not like him.

The house was dark when she arrived home, leading Izzy to believe that her father was not there. She entered through the kitchen door, crossed to the hallway and went upstairs. A light snore broke the silence when she reached the second floor. On tiptoe, she crept to her father's door and cracked it open just enough to peek inside. The room looked eerie in the low glow from the small lamp on the nightstand. An empty bottle of Jameson whiskey lay on the floor beside a used shot glass.

It wasn't like him to drink whiskey. For a large man, it was one of the few drinks that humbled him. Searching her memory, she could only recall two instances when he had fallen to the urges of whiskey. The day her mother died and the day she told him she was accepted to university. You would have thought that her leaving for school was going to be the death of him, she thought with a sigh as she shook her head.

Izzy stepped into his room, walked over to the bed and lifted the leg that hung haphazardly off the side. After removing his shoes, she tugged the blanket up over him and gathered the ancient family bible from his hand. He didn't move. The heavy rise and fall of his chest informed her that he was in a deep alcohol-induced sleep. She stared at the bible in her hand. Whatever tortured his thoughts had to be bad for him to turn to the scripture for guidance. Not that her father wasn't a God-fearing man, it just wasn't common place for him to turn to the bible for answers.

As she opened the nightstand drawer to return the book to its place, the edge of something sticking out of the pages caught her eye. She opened the bible to the page where the slender, aged parchment lay hidden. The parchment looked too fragile to touch. It wasn't folded. It rested on the page as if it were meant to be there. Izzy held her breath, afraid that if she breathed too hard, the parchment would turn to dust and blow away. Careful not to wake her father, she laid the book open on the nightstand under the lamp.

It wasn't something she recognized. Where had it come from? Had it been in the bible forever and she hadn't known it? Who put it there? Questions poured through her brain as she studied the parchment. The words were written in the old language of Gaelic.

Damn, she wished she'd studied that when she had the chance. Izzy hurried to her room, grabbed a pad and pen off her desk and returned without a sound to her father's bedside. Though her hand shook, she was careful not to miss one letter and spelled the words exactly as she read them. As if the low snore wasn't enough of a sign, a sideways glance reassured her thoughts that her father was out for the night. He lay, flat on his back, sprawled under the blanket and his head was tilted to the side on his pillow.

After closing the bible, she tucked it in the nightstand drawer, switched off the light and left the room, shutting the door behind her. Did her father's drinking binge and this parchment have anything to do with the meeting earlier? Izzy couldn't be sure. It could just be coincidence that he'd downed a whole bottle of whiskey and pulled the family bible out. Wasn't it a known fact that when some people drank, God's word became their best friend? She shook her head. Her father wasn't like that. He seldom drank whiskey due to the way his system reacted to it…instant drunk.

It was obvious something bothered him, but what? She stared at the words she'd written on her notepad. She didn't remember seeing this in the bible before. Had it been there and she just didn't notice it, or had her father hidden it somewhere else and placed it in the bible tonight?

Izzy couldn't be sure. That bible wasn't something she had ever been allowed to touch very often. As far as she knew, it had always been in the safety of that nightstand drawer in her parents' room. She wondered why. Was it because of this conglomeration of gibberish on her notepad that the family bible was kept hidden? Or was that just the place her mother had wanted it when she was alive?

Either way, it didn't matter. What did was the fact that she sat on her bed, staring at words she couldn't understand. There wasn't a muscle that didn't ache in her arms, back and neck. It had been a long time since she'd pitched in and worked as a waitress during one of her father's darts tournaments. She was definitely out of practice and out of shape for carrying a full tray of ale filled mugs.

What a night. She sighed as she lay back on her bed. Too tired to think straight anymore, Izzy placed the notepad on the nightstand, kicked off her shoes, wiggled out of her clothes, then settled naked under the covers for the night.

Tomorrow, she'd find out what those words meant. And just maybe, she'd get her father to talk, but she couldn't count on it. Cornering a bushy-eyebrowed, redheaded farm boy was her better bet.

* * * * *

In the early morning hours, he crept through the darkened streets of London. The stench of burned flesh and hair lingered, but no longer made him wretch. Instead, it

45

fueled his hatred. *The MacKinnon had beaten him* repeated in his head, becoming a silent reminder of his failure. He allowed himself a low snarl, even though it caused his left cheek to crack. Renewed pain sizzled down his neck, along his arm and to his fingertips.

With the help of his powers, he had controlled and limited the amount of flames that had touched his skin. But the cottage fire had been great and his system had been weakened by his fight with the MacKinnon. Injuries were sustained, and though he tried, his magic could not cure all that was wrong. He needed help if he wanted to regain his strength and refuel his magic.

It had taken him longer than anticipated to reach his city hideout. The car he had stolen had no air conditioning. Due to the heat of the sun tormenting his tortured flesh, he hid in cool locations by day and was limited to traveling at night. Not knowing if he was being followed made him careful in his actions. He did not wish to lead his enemies to his lair. After recovering the key to his flat from behind the loose brick in the wall to the right of the stoop, Leod unlocked the door, pocketed the key and slipped inside without a sound.

He flipped on the light and hissed at the instant brightness. Once the pain in his left eye subsided, he forced both eyes opened, removed the hood of the dark cloak he wore and examined his facial injuries in the hallway mirror. The eye itself was functioning, but the eyebrow was missing. It had burned off during the fire. Running a fingertip across the tender skin, he wondered if it would grow back.

The first layer of skin was charred pink and had already begun to peel. Areas of his cheek, ear and neck were visibly marred, giving the appearance of melted wax. This could be used to his advantage. He smirked at his new face. If the hair on the side of his head grew back, he could cover part of the marred ear and cheek. Without the eyebrow, it added eeriness to the golden wheat color of his eyes and made him look dangerous or crazy.

He nodded as he stared at his reflection. This he would turn to his advantage. The MacKinnon may have ruined his boyish good looks, but this new design gave him an edge in his abilities to control his men. One look at the damage and they'd believe that his enemy was their enemy. If the MacKinnon wrought such pain and disfigurement on their leader, one of great power, as he had led them to believe, then what would this enemy do to them?

Though his cheek burned and his eye watered, a wicked smile cracked his face.

Inch by slow inch, he eased his arm out of the makeshift sling he made and flexed his fist. During the fight, the blast that occurred and the fire, his shoulder was dislocated. Dislocations were typical for his injured joint, so putting it back in place had not been a problem. As a kid, he knocked it out of joint and scared others with the loose hanging arm just for fun. The memory of the horror on one young man's face in particular made him laugh. What a jerk that kid had been, he remembered. But that jerk was easy to control.

Leod walked down the hall and into the kitchen. He picked up the phone and dialed. As soon as the man on the other end said, "hello," he spoke.

"It's me. I made it. Get Doc and be here within the hour." Without another word, he hung up.

Yep, he decided as he poured himself a drink. That jerk was the best minion a dark wizard could ask for.

* * * * *

A stale musty odor tickled her nose. When she stepped forward, cobwebs fluttered across her cheek, making her shudder. Swallowing the urge to scream, she brushed them from her face. Goose bumps traversed her arms and she rubbed vigorously in an attempt to warm herself, but failed. The air around her was damp and cool. Izzy blinked and cleared her vision, but it didn't help. She didn't recognize her surroundings.

Where was she and how did she get there? No matter which direction she looked, she was unable to gain her bearings or determine her location. Low light gave the room a gray appearance. Wooden shelves lined the walls. The floor was nothing more than compacted earth. Thick layers of dust, cobwebs and dirt coated every bottle on the shelves. A swirl of dust filtered in the air as she lifted one from its place, causing her to cough.

No label was visible when she scraped away a layer of crust. The bottle contained a liquid, but what it was she could not tell. The bottle's shape and the way that it was capped implied a liquor of some sort. Being raised in a bar, she'd seen plenty of liquor bottles and could probably name what was inside without looking at the label, simply by the color and shape of the bottle. But the ones in this room looked ancient. Izzy replaced the bottle to its spot and rubbed her dirty hands on her pant legs.

Déjà vu filtered through her system. The place seemed familiar. But why? Had she been there before? Unable to remember, Izzy searched for an exit. A rickety ladder led to the ceiling and what appeared to be a trap door. Was she in a cellar? Was this room's ceiling the floor of the room above? One shake of the ladder and she was certain it wouldn't hold her weight. Without any other visible way out, she placed a foot on the bottom rung.

After whispering a prayer that the ladder would hold, she stepped up. Slow and steady, she eased from one rung to another. Halfway up, a rung gave way. Splinters stabbed into her palms as she clung to the ladder while her legs flailed beneath her. Before she could land a foot on a supportive spot, the wood snapped, sending her spiraling to the ground.

As the dust cleared, Izzy sat up coughing and gagging, gasping for air. Her back hurt. Her palms held tiny slivers of wood beneath her skin and all she wanted was out. Out of this place, with its spiders, dirt, broken ladder and walls full of bottles. As she eased onto her knees, she grabbed a large wooden barrel for support. Its surface was cool and it felt heavy and full, giving her the counterbalance that she needed to stand.

On her feet, she could see behind the barrel. There seemed to be a slender gap in the wall. Izzy grasped the barrel. With each push, the splinters in her hands buried deeper, shooting pain up her arms. Izzy sucked in a breath, gritted her teeth and shoved with all her might, toppling the barrel onto its side. This made it easy to roll out of the way. A small round hole appeared that was situated low in the wall near the ground.

Where it led, she did not know and at this point she didn't care. She just wanted out. On all fours, Izzy forced herself into the hole and pushed until she fell through to the other side. She tumbled onto her shoulder and rolled onto her back.

A bright flash blinded her. She shielded her eyes with her arm and blinked to focus as she scurried onto her knees. Not able to determine what caused the brightness, she inched away from the light, until something hard and cold stopped her progress. Several seconds seemed like an eternity before her vision adjusted and her mother appeared. Izzy froze.

It couldn't be, she gasped. Her mother had been dead for years. And yet, here she was, standing within two feet of her. Izzy couldn't help but stare at the transparent, petite figure of her mother. All fear lifted from Izzy's soul when her mother's spirit smiled. It was a smile that had always soothed her in the past and didn't fail to do so at that moment. The warmth of her mother's love wrapped around her, even though they did not touch. Her mother lifted a transparent index finger to her lips as she said, "Shush, my little one. Our secret."

Before Izzy could respond, her mother's spirit disappeared. Jumping upright, her head hit a hard object and stars shot behind her closed eyelids. She spun around on her heels as she opened her eyes. Her jaw dropped at the sight behind her. A solid rock statue of a man, dressed in a kilt and holding a sword in a battle stance, met her gaze. The visible bare chest was well muscled, making her ache to touch him and explore his body. His face was chiseled and handsome. When she lifted her gaze to his eyes, she jumped backward and stumbled.

The air left her lungs in a whish as the room darkened and spun around her.

Within a matter of seconds, Izzy sat on the floor beside her bed, wrapped in a blanket and rubbing the lump on her head. What the hell happened? Her head spun as she tried to sort through her muddled thoughts. It had to have been a dream, she decided.

"Damn," she muttered as she crawled back into bed, "that was some dream."

But was it a dream? She knew it had to be, but it seemed so real. Her mother, the room, the statue, the images of each in her head ignited a smidgeon of doubt and had her second-guessing the possibility. Had she been there before? Izzy tucked the blanket around her and settled back onto her pillow.

She examined her palms for splinters, but found none. The lump on her head she was certain she got from the corner of the nightstand when she rolled out of bed. But why had she fallen out of bed? She wasn't drunk.

The vision of those stone-cold eyes burned bright inside her head, stalling her breath for a second. It had been the sight of those eyes that had caused her to stumble in her dream. Was the sensation of falling backward in the dream so strong that she'd tossed and turned in her bed until she rolled right out? That had to be it, she tried to convince herself. Those eyes hadn't scared her. She'd just stumbled in her dream. The fear of falling was what made her roll out of bed. That had to be it, she reiterated to herself.

Though she tried to go back to sleep, she had difficulty doing so. Those eyes appeared each time she closed her eyes, causing her to open them and stare at the ceiling. In an attempt to rid her conscious of those stone-cold orbs, she forced her focus on the room that was in her dream. It reminded her of somewhere she felt in her gut that she had been in before. But when? Where? And what did her mother have to do with it?

It had been a long time since she'd dreamt of her mother. Tonight's reappearance of her mother in her dream made Izzy ache for one of the world's greatest hugs, her mother's hugs. Good, strong hugs and a beautiful smile were the two things Izzy remembered most of her mother. But what did her mother have to do with that room or that statue or this dream, for that matter?

Izzy punched her pillow. It annoyed her that she couldn't think straight.

For some reason, her mother had appeared in this dream. But why? Both eyes closed as she tried to sort out her thoughts. The memory of the warmth of her mother's love enveloping her made her shiver. The thought of her mother's smile brought a slight smile to her own lips. But it was the sound of her mother's words replaying in her head that made her sit upright.

Shush, my little one. Our secret.

What secret? Exasperated, Izzy flopped back on the pillow. What did a secret, her mother and a statue have in common?

Not just any statue. That annoying inner voice seemed to whisper. This was all too confusing. She sighed as she rolled onto her side. Then it hit her. The statue resembled the Scottish god of a man from her dreams. The strong arms, the broad chest, great legs and the large sword that she saw in her prior visions did seem similar to the male statue in tonight's dream. Though she tried, she couldn't remember his eyes as she scrolled through her thoughts. In the dream tonight, the statue's eyes were stone-cold and emotionless.

Emotionless. She swallowed hard. The man in her dreams never responded to her sexual advances. He just sat there, stone-cold...emotionless. Just once, she wished he'd react to her touch and their bodies would connect in a wild night of sex. But for some reason, that dream never changed. He never moved. His features never softened when she caressed his cheek and his eyes...try as she might, she couldn't remember his eyes.

Unable to ignore the growing throb from the lump on her head, Izzy gave up on sleep. One glance out the window and she knew it was early morning. The sun's rays were peeking across the sky, pushing back the night.

Might as well get up, she sighed. She yanked the covers back, swung her legs over the edge and stood. Dizziness did not occur as she feared it might due to the size of the goose egg on her head. Instead, it just provided her skull with a dull ache and worsened when she touched it.

"Gotta remember not to do that," Izzy stated, jerking her hand from the lump.

After putting on a robe, she went down the hall to check on her dad. The door was cracked open. The bed was bodiless and unmade. The empty shot glass and liquor bottle were gone. Izzy hurried downstairs, hoping to talk with her dad, but he was nowhere to be found. The bottle was in the trash and the glass was in the dish drain, washed and left to dry. She searched every room, then looked outside and realized his car was gone. This wasn't like him at all. His head had to be hurting him after drinking an entire bottle of whiskey.

The last time he consumed that much alcohol, he didn't budge for three days.

Izzy shook her head as she returned upstairs. Something wasn't right with him. She bet it had to do with last night's meeting of the gentlemen's club or the ancient script she found in the bible.

Not sure why she did it, Izzy looked over her shoulder as if checking to see if anyone was watching, then went into her dad's room and over to the nightstand. Again, she made sure that her dad was not in eyesight and pulled open the drawer.

Izzy's jaw dropped. Though she suspected it, seeing it only added to the confusion.

Not only was her dad missing, so was the family bible.

What was he up too? Izzy turned on her heels, went to her room, gathered her laptop and the notepad, then marched downstairs to the kitchen. She needed a cup of coffee to wake up and clear her head. If this was a computer problem, she'd have it fixed in no time. But this was her dad. Something was bothering him and it irked her not to know what it was. Without knowing what bothered him, she wouldn't be able to help him fix the problem.

After setting up the coffeepot to brew, she plopped into a chair at the table and ticked off the list of things in her head that she thought might be at the base of the problem. First, there was the fire that leveled one of his rental properties. That could have him on edge, but she doubted it. Replacing the cottage wouldn't be a top priority or concern due to the fact that their village wasn't a high tourist region.

Second, there was that unusual meeting of the gentlemen's group during one of his dart tournaments. That definitely wasn't a normal occurrence, not when he took his duties as the master of ceremonies so seriously. She stood and poured herself a cup of coffee. Her father's absence wasn't normal, Izzy decided. He had to be up to something, but what? She returned to her seat with cup in hand and stared across its rim.

The vision of a handsome man and a plain-Jane popped into her head. Was he the missing Brother Leod who rented the cottage? Did they set the fire and flee the scene with Ned's help?

"Nah," Izzy said out loud. That couldn't be it. She saw Ned come out of that meeting with the rest of the men. He was her dad's best friend. There was no way Ned would do anything dishonest. It wasn't in his nature. Gambling was, and try as she might, she couldn't recall seeing him at the darts tournament for long.

Now that truly was unusual. Then again, it was busy. He could have been there and she missed him somehow, though she doubted it. Izzy took a sip of her coffee, then set up her computer. If she was lucky, the internet connection from home would work and she'd translate the Celtic message she found in the bible. Maybe it had something to do with the reason for her dad's strange behavior.

The connection at home was slower than at the pub, but usable as Izzy logged on. It did not take her long to locate a Celtic to English dictionary site and translate the words.

'Tis a hearty place ta be.
Wenches above ye.
Spirits around thee.
Aged comfort cradles he of which ye seek.
Thy second hand is just beneath.
Roll thy barrel 'n take a peek.

What the hell? It made no sense to her, no matter what language it was in. Izzy sat back and stared at the words on the notepad. Just last night she dreamt of rolling a barrel to escape. Odd that occurred in her vision and now appeared in this...this riddle. She decided to call it that for the lack of a better term for the mash of words in an un-decipherable paragraph.

"Okay, talk this through, Izzy girl," she said to herself as she stood and paced.

"What started this chain of strangeness?"

One pass, then two around the kitchen table before she stopped dead still.

It had to be those two in the pub, handsome hunky monk and plain-Jane.

Izzy logged out of her computer and shut it down. Willy had said that he thought plain-Jane might be the niece of the woman who bought the old Castle MacKinnon. A glance at the clock, and she knew it was still too early to pop in on the owner of the castle for a visit. But it wasn't too early to find Colin. She smiled as she scooted upstairs to shower and dress.

If there was one person besides her dad she could depend on, it was Colin. And right now, she depended on his inability to keep anything from her.

Chapter Five

ℬ

Bright sunlight reflected off a metallic object in the distance as she rounded a curve in the road near Colin's home. Squinting, she saw what looked to be Ned's car turning onto the roadway leading to Colin's family sheep farm.

Last night she sensed that Colin was up to something along with her dad, Ned and that group from the gentlemen's club. Seeing Ned's car headed to Colin's farm this morning added to her suspicions. There was a mystery brewing and for the first time in the year and a half since she'd been home from university, her synapses sizzled with a challenge.

Everyday life in a small Scottish village was boring. But not today. She grinned. The men were up to something and she was on to their game. Were they after an arsonist? A wayward monk with a taste for a plain-Jane of a woman, or was it something else? Her blood seemed to hum with excitement as it flowed through her veins. It took great restraint not to floor the accelerator and catch up to the car she had seen turn down the road ahead. As she got closer, a smidgeon of doubt tainted her confidence. Was she sure the car she followed was Ned's? What if it turned out to be someone else? A half laugh, half snort escaped on a heavy breath.

Izzy bit her lip as she glanced at her reflection in the rearview mirror. It wasn't uncommon for her to drop by Colin's for a visit. Everyone knew they were close and she'd spent many a days on this farm with Colin. Hell, she knew every inch of this farm as well as he did and could shear a sheep with the best of them.

She swallowed hard and forced her doubts to the back of her mind. No, that was Ned's car and she knew it. Were they having another meeting of the gentlemen's club?

Her eyebrow arched as a new idea sprang to life. Right now, they didn't know she was on to them and that element was on her side. Before she got close enough to the farmhouse to be seen, Izzy pulled her car into a grove of trees and hid it as best as possible.

Careful not to make noise, she worked her way toward the house. She peeked around a haystack, then scooted to a large boulder. The sheep farm was in one of the higher elevations that led into the Grampian Mountains. Rocks, grass, trees and wildflowers were plentiful. It made feeding the sheep easy for Colin and his family. Herding them was the trick. Memories of her and Colin spending hours after school stalking the occasional wayward sheep with the help of the dogs trained to herd popped into her head. They'd spent hours in their youth, playing and working on this farm. The sound of the sheep and the dogs off in the distance made her smile.

Closer and closer she crept until she was securely hidden behind the hedges underneath the kitchen window. Lucky for her, the window was open. This was crazy, she chided herself mentally. What if she was seen? How would she explain this? Determination set in and settled the uneasiness that tainted her system. She squared her shoulders and decided she'd just have to make sure that she wasn't seen. Izzy bit her lip and craned her neck as she strained to hear the conversation inside.

Mumbled male voices drifted to her ears, but the words were difficult to distinguish. Stretching closer to the window sill, she attempted to gain a better position without being caught. A quick glance through the hedges and she saw the yard remained empty. The doors on the barn were closed.

On tiptoe, she peeked over the sill from the left lower corner of the window. Ned sat with his back to her. Colin stood, leaning against the counter near the stove and to her surprise, she found her dad. He sat to the right of Ned, but at an angle he probably wouldn't notice her unless he was looking directly out the window. Because she had not seen his car in the driveway, she decided that he must have ridden with Ned.

Izzy took a deep breath and forced her breathing to slow. They were up to something and she needed to remain as quiet as possible if she wanted to hear anything.

"Colin, I trust you to keep this quiet. No blabbing to Isabo. I'll not have her involved." She heard her dad say.

"Aye, sir," Colin replied. "I've never told her of the society and see no reason to include her in our affairs. I'm concerned with the fact that she joined some website that had the name of this missing Brother Leod associated with it. It could be dangerous."

"Keep a close eye on her. Don't let her follow up on it. Find some way to get her to drop it."

Izzy fought the urge to climb through the window and let them know that she needed no man to keep tabs on her, especially not Colin. How dare her dad decide what she should and shouldn't do? Gritting her teeth, she forced a calm she did not feel to settle her anger to a low sizzle. What was her dad up to that he didn't want her help, but chose Colin's instead? A twinge of hurt simmered in her gut.

And what was this society that Colin mentioned? Maybe it was the name of their gentlemen's club, which she'd known met at her dad's tavern for years. If the meetings were supposed to be a secret, none of them had kept that one.

Out of the corner of her eye, she saw the edge of her family's bible. Ned was bent over it and it looked to her as if he was studying a passage from it. But her instincts told her he wasn't reading the book. Nay, she knew he was looking at the ancient parchment containing the riddle.

Her suspicions were verified when he sat upright and stated the paragraph, word for word as she had translated it earlier. When he leaned back, she caught a glimpse of a piece of paper he handed to her dad. He must have been working on translating the verse.

"Are you certain that's what it says?"

"Aye," Ned replied. "It's a riddle. You both know the tale. The brothers were cursed and hidden. Their sister, Akira, had their statues hidden by men from trusted clans. Until now, we all thought it was a myth. The proof has been given to us. We must step up and honor our forefathers promise. We have to decipher this to find the brother they were given to hide. It is our responsibility to show the rest of the society that this is real. There are clansmen in need of our help."

At the moment, Izzy wasn't sure which startled her more. The words that came out of Ned's mouth or the fact that this was the most she'd ever heard him say at one time. He spoke of proof that the myth was real. Could the men in her life possibly believe in this tale? Brothers cursed and turned to stone, was that even possible? From the sound of the conversation as she continued to eavesdrop, they believed and for some reason they were bound to help these clansmen.

Colin's voice drifted to her ears. "Well then, let's break it down line by line. 'Tis a hearty place ta be. What during their time was considered a hearty place? What year were they cursed?" Colin asked.

"Around 1740," Angus added after he cleared his throat. "And hearty could mean just about anything. It might be a place where the clans met."

"I doubt it," Ned interjected on a snort. "Not with the next line being, *wenches above ye.*"

"They had whorehouses back then?"

Izzy slapped her hand over her mouth to stifle the laugh that she had to swallow at Colin's surprised tone. Didn't he know that was the world's oldest profession? When her dad spoke the next line out loud, her heart skipped a beat.

Spirits around thee, repeated in her head.

Where had she seen a spirit? In her dream, the spirit of her mother visited her. Or did it mean spirits as in drink?

Aged comfort, echoed in her head as the rest of the words of that sentence momentarily fell on deaf ears. In her world, aged comfort came stored in a bottle and in the form of a good Scottish brew. The older the better, she remembered her grandfather saying. *Cradles he of whom ye seek*, the rest of that sentence teased her thoughts as she tuned out the men in the background.

The words of the riddle were shooting through her thoughts at a rapid rate. *Thy second hand is just beneath.* Was this about one of the so-called MacKinnon brothers?

As a young girl, her mother once told her the tale of the brothers who were turned to stone. It made her sad, so her mother never told her again. Instead, she created a story of a young woman who would one day find her eternal love and free him from his solitary world. Was it the same story, just twisted with a happy ending to make a young child smile? Had her mother done that? Izzy closed her eyes and the visions from last nights dream reappeared.

Roll thy barrel 'n take a peek. Both eyes widened as the strength left her legs and she slowly slid down the wall onto her knees. It hit her hard. She knew she had seen that barrel before and she knew in her gut she had been in that room. But its exact location wouldn't surface, no matter how hard she tried to recall the memory. Something kept it blocked.

Not knowing why she couldn't think straight had Izzy confused. If the men found her, how would she explain this? Drawing on her inner strength, she forced her legs to work and stood, but kept away from the window. She had to get out of there without being seen. It took great concentration to work her way back to her car and leave without being caught, but she managed.

Not one part of the drive back into town focused in her head. It wasn't until she sat in the car, with the motor running, that she realized she was in front of her dad's tavern. In slow motion, she lifted her gaze to the cornerstone. Etched for all to see, if they actually looked, was the date of the original building. 1664 seemed to glare back at her from the ancient block.

Her dad had said that the brothers were cursed in 1740. Could one of them have been hidden inside of the tavern? If her dad, Ned and Colin were like their ancestors, the probability was high that they would have hidden him in a place of public drinking and gaming. Depending on if the curse was real, and she wasn't saying that it was, but if it was, then it made sense to her that her ancestors would have hidden one of the brothers in the tavern.

Izzy dug her key to the tavern out of the glove compartment of her car. After checking to see if her dad was returning, she slid out of her car, walked to the door and entered. She made sure to lock the door behind her.

There was no way she was going to start serving drinks to customers. If the door was left unlocked, she knew that would most likely happen. It wasn't uncommon for the older men in town to drop in and spend the day, drinking and telling tales. But not today. She stiffened her spine and stared around the room. Even the patrons of the Internet Pub were going to have to suffer for a while.

For today, she had mission. Find a man of stone.

* * * * *

An hour passed and she had no luck in finding the hidden room from her dream. The sensation of having been in it before refused to leave her system. Instead, it hovered on the edge of her gray matter as if teasing her with its secret. Izzy bit her lip as she settled on a stool with her back against the bar, scanning the room for something she had to have missed.

Line by line, she went over the riddle in her head. She stared up at the second floor. That level had once been inn rooms. The upstairs was no longer used as nightly rental rooms since the tourist traffic had slowed many years prior. Portions of this room were part of the original establishment, but a good bit of it had been refurbished over the years.

"Wenches above thee, cradled by aged mead, the one ye seek is just beneath." Izzy whispered. The answer hit her.

"Oh my God, you're an idiot." She chided herself. In one swift movement, she was on her feet and rounding the bar.

The women of her heritage would never have allowed a whore upstairs. Izzy decided. The wenches mentioned had to have been barmaids. As she tugged open the trapdoor in the floor behind the bar that led down to the cellar, a chill shot down her spine and her arms covered in goose bumps. Was it caused by the sudden, cool updraft that came from the cellar? It had to be. Izzy rubbed her arms in an attempt to warm them, then reached under the bar and switched on the light downstairs.

With each step down, a strange sensation slithered through her veins. Was she really on to something or was she just imagining the odd pull in her gut? Cases of mead, scotch and beer lined the cool brick walls of the room. Izzy walked from one end to the other, searching for something, but she wasn't sure what. Then she stopped dead in her tracks. This room seemed smaller than the area upstairs. Why hadn't she ever noticed this before? *Because you weren't looking for a secret room before*, she silently reminded herself.

She paced in a straight line from the one side of the room to the other. Izzy scooted upstairs and walked from one end of the room to the other. It confirmed her suspicions. The room downstairs was shorter by several feet. Ten to twelve if her calculations were right. She studied the placement of the walls, then hurried back into the cellar.

The back wall seemed to come short of the upstairs wall. But was it uncommon for cellars to be a good deal smaller than the actual building? Though she couldn't be sure, she decided that in this case, it wasn't. The hidden room had to be somewhere along that back wall.

Slowly and deliberately, she examined each brick, inched every barrel away from the wall and shifted every bottle on the shelves. No opening appeared. Discouraged and tired, she plopped onto the steps and sat with her elbows on her knees and her chin resting in her hands. She had to be missing something. It had to be along that back wall. It just had to be. On a heavy sigh, she leaned against the brick wall that lined the stairwell.

Her shoulder sank. Izzy bolted upright. There was an indention in the area where her body had touched the wall. It was the size of one brick. When she pressed, the brick slid about an inch further, then stopped. She ran her fingertips along the brick, but found nothing. As she searched, she found a notch the size of her finger along the brick to the right of the one that moved.

The breath stilled in her lungs. What had she found? Afraid that the old brick might crumble, she slid her finger in the grove, slow and easy, then tugged lightly. Her teeth sank into her lower lip and sweat beaded upon her forehead.

What was she getting so nervous over? She was a modern woman, a computer whiz. Her intellect told her that curses did not exist, but a little voice inside her head whispered, *what if it did*?

The brick to the right turned as if it were on a pivot of some sort. A grate of brick upon brick echoed. Dust rose and thickened the air as a section of the shelves to the right of the stairs vibrated. Izzy coughed and gagged, and covered her eyes with the back of her hand until the dust cleared.

After several seconds, Izzy was able to focus. A few steps to the right of the stairs, the wall had turned, shelves and all. It reminded her of a scene from an old movie, where the lead actor leaned against the wall, it spun around and he fell through to the hidden room. In another situation, she would have found that funny, but at the moment it was her reality and not a movie scene. Her legs trembled with each step. Her mouth dried and her heart pounded. Was the proof that the curse was real on the other side of that wall?

Izzy took a deep breath and applied force to the wall. No amount of pressure made it turn any further. It was stuck, or that was as far as it went, she decided with a shrug of her shoulders. The opening was slender, but she managed to wiggle her way through to the other side. Cold, dark and damp had her wishing for a jacket and a flashlight. Remembering that her father kept a couple of flashlights under the bar in case of power outages, she shimmied back through the tight gap, hurried up the stairs, grabbed the first one she saw, checked it to make sure it worked and resumed her search.

Every muscle tensed and her mouth dropped open as the light filled the small room. She couldn't believe her eyes. It was the same as in her dream. Ancient bottles covered in dirt lined the shelves. Several large barrels were along one wall. And at the far end, a rickety ladder led up to what appeared to be a trap door.

This was unreal. It couldn't be. But with each stilted step she took, she knew she had been in this room before. She couldn't remember when, but her gut instinct was never wrong. As she stood at the base of the ladder, she panned the light across the trap door. If her direction was right, she was under her dad's office. Closing her eyes, she visualized his office in her head. The door had to be under the antique liquor cabinet that stood against the wall.

A vague memory of playing hide-and-seek as a child resurfaced. She and Colin had been playing in the bar. Try as she might, only scattered remnants of the day came back to her. One minute she remembered hiding and the next she was being found by her dad in the bottom of the cabinet, asleep. Had she hidden so well that Colin didn't find her and she fell asleep? Or had something else happened?

Shush, our secret, seemed to whisper in the air, startling Izzy as she scanned the room for the source of the sound.

Turning on her heels, she froze when the light landed on a memorable barrel. It stood exactly where it had in her dream. Izzy took a deep breath. Why did she know this room? On shaky legs, she moved toward the barrel. At first it looked as if it sat snug against the wall. On closer inspection, she noticed a gap behind it. From what she could see, there was a hole in the wall directly behind the barrel. But she was too large to wiggle between the barrel and the wall.

A small child could, but she couldn't. Izzy straightened. Why had she thought that? Had she been in here as a child? Shaking her head, she tried to focus on the matter at hand…getting behind that barrel.

She balanced the light on the closest shelf, then concentrated on tipping the barrel. If she turned it on its side, then she could roll it. Just like in the dream, the realization hit her, causing her to pause for a moment. How did she know this place? One tug and she knew the barrel was full.

She wondered what two hundred year old mead tasted like. Just imagining Colin's expression over this discovery put a smile on her face. The man did like his mead. She laughed as she shook her head and gathered her strength. This would be much easier if it was empty. Too bad he wasn't around to remedy that situation for her. Instead, she'd have to do it the old fashioned way. Izzy planted her feet as she placed her back against the barrel and used her leg muscles to help tilt the barrel over.

Once it was on its side, she didn't need to move it any further. It was far enough out of the way that she could fit through the opening. Grabbing the flashlight, Izzy wiggled into the hole in the wall on her hands and knees and tumbled through to the other side with a thud. But she didn't lose her grip on the flashlight. Izzy lifted to her knees, ran the back of her hand across her eyes to clear the dirt and blinked to focus.

Her chest tightened, the air stilled in her lungs and her jaw dropped open as she lifted the light. A tall solid form of rock graced her eyes. Muscled legs, kilt draped around his waist to his knees, no shirt covered his broad, phenomenal chest. Thick biceps were flexed taut, while both hands gripped the largest sword that she had ever seen. His stance reminded her of the pictures she had seen of ancient Scottish warriors during battle, as they prepared to lunge at their opponents. Only this warrior never made contact, instead his image was frozen in what was once a huge boulder or rock. At least that's what she kept telling herself. This wasn't a man cursed. This was a work of a long forgotten, talented sculptor.

Uhm, the things she wanted to do if this were a real man. A chill shot down her spine as she licked her lips, wishing for a peek beneath his kilt. If all of him were proportionate to his large build, then he would be a challenge to enjoy. Would he taste salty or sweet? Absently, she traced the lower edge of his kilt and smiled. Oh, how she wished this man existed. There was no doubt in her mind that his cock would be larger and better than any she'd ever imagined.

Unable to pull her gaze away, she perused the man of stone until a tiny object caught her eye and she froze. In the crook of his arm sat Melinda, the doll that Izzy lost when she was young. Uncounted moments slipped away before Izzy found the strength to move. She took a deep breath and inched forward until she was within arms length of her doll. On tiptoe, she reached for the precious item of her youth.

For the first time since she was about seven years old, she held Melinda to her chest. Tears filled her eyes as she looked up at the cold, colorless eyes of the giant man frozen in stone. Somehow she found this room when she was a child and left her favorite doll on his arm. The image of his face with the colorless eyes, his body in its ferocious stance and his sword drawn in attack mode were tattooed within the hidden chambers of her mind and only appeared in her dreams. But why? How? Her hand shook as she cupped his cheek.

"Thank you for taking care of her," she whispered, though she wasn't sure why she said it. Heat warmed her palm, causing her to jerk her hand away. Flexing her hand in front of her face, she stared in disbelief. Had the sensation of heat been real or was it simply a reaction to her overactive libido? Never before had touching a statue ever caused her hand to warm as it had just now.

No, it had to be her imagination, she decided. Reaching to touch the stone creation's face again, she was startled by a sound reverberating through the hole behind her.

"Isabo, are you in there, lass."

Chapter Six

એ

Izzy stumbled backward, then stiffened upright. It wouldn't do to have them find her frazzled over an old stuffed doll and a fantastic Scottish laird carved in stone. That wasn't her style. Gothic tough chick was, so she straightened her shoulders and tilted her chin. Looking up, she swore she saw her mother's face and heard the whisper of "*'Tis time to set him free,*" from her lips. If she hadn't seen the figment of her imagination's mouth move, she wouldn't have believed it. As it was, she wasn't sure she trusted her own eyes or the ability of her own hands to work correctly. The transparent image disappeared as quickly as it appeared, making her think she was seeing things.

She blinked, then forced herself to focus. One glance around the room and she knew that it was built to house the statue and not much more. There was no other way in or out other than through the hole in the wall. And nobody else was in there with her.

Clutching the doll to her chest, she maneuvered back through the hole, leaving the flashlight behind, turned on and pointed directly at the statue. It was the only way she would have to prove to the men that she was not insane. She found a stone carving of a man hidden in an unknown chamber of their cellar. How it got there, she didn't know, but she intended to find out. It had to have been placed there first and then the wall was built around it.

Was it a MacKinnon? Did this prove that the curse was real? Part of her wanted to believe that the gorgeous stone man was real, but she doubted it. As she tumbled through the hole and landed at their feet, strong hands grabbed her and helped her up.

"Are you all right, child?" Concern filled her dad's voice as he drew her into a bear hug.

"How did you find me?"

"You did not hide your tracks very well at all." Ned quipped, with a nod of his head toward the turning section of wall that she found earlier.

It surprised her how much more open it was at the moment. Obviously, the men forced it wider to accommodate their size than she had. And where they stood was where she left the barrel, which they had rolled out of the way. Instead of rejoicing in finding a barrel of two hundred year old mead as she had suspected he would, Colin was on his knees behind her with half his body stuck through the hole.

"Looks like Izzy found our MacKinnon," he said as he pulled out of the hole. "And a mighty interesting barrel," he added with a wag of his thick red eyebrows.

Izzy shook her head as she lifted her gaze to her dad's.

"You want to tell me why you are down here and how you know the location of our friend in there?"

She opened her mouth to speak, but closed it just as fast. To tell the truth, she wasn't exactly sure how she found him or if the statue was truly "a him" at all. Glancing from man to man, she suspected that they thought the curse was real even if she wasn't sure. When Ned got up from looking through the hole, his face said it all as he nodded his head while staring at her dad. He believed that the statue was a MacKinnon, thus the other two agreed.

Were they right or had they lost their minds? A residual sensation of warmth lingered in her palm, making her uncertain of her own sanity at the moment. There was no reasoning behind what happened when she touched that statue or the appearance of her mother's image, *if* she had even experienced those things at all.

Izzy stepped out of her dad's reach and returned his steady gaze.

"I think it's time we talk and you men tell me the truth about what's going on."

Before anyone could say anything, she turned on her heels and marched from the room. The more she tried to determine how or why she seemed to know that room existed, the more her head hurt. Melinda in her hand was proof that she had somehow been there before as a child. But why had she left her most prized possession behind? And why couldn't she remember visiting that hidden space behind the wall?

Izzy settled on the first stool as she rounded the bar. She held her doll in both hands with her arms rested on the bar and her feet hitched in the lower rungs. Melinda was one of a kind made specifically for her by her mother. Slowly and delicately, she fingered the blue jean coveralls of the homemade doll. Haphazard red yarn pigtails hung loose, tied by slender green ribbons. Her once bright, hand-painted face now was faded with age, but still sported a mischievous smile and a pair of blue eyes.

I made her in your image, a tomboy for my tomboy. She heard her mother's voice inside her head as if she still stood near. A tear slid down her cheek. In her little girl world, her mother was the most wonderful, gentle woman to have ever lived.

"I see you found Melinda," her dad said as he rounded the bar and sat beside her. "Any idea how she got there?"

The knot in her throat refused to allow her to speak, so she simply shook her head. Colin let the trapdoor shut with a slam, causing her to jump and snap back to reality. Now was not the time for this, she reprimanded herself as she swallowed hard and forced herself to pull it together.

"I..." she started, stopped, cleared her throat, then started again, "I want to know the truth. What is this all about? Who do you think put that statue down there and what makes you think that that is one of the supposed MacKinnon brothers turned to stone in that myth?"

Izzy watched her dad's face. From the swipe of his large hand across his forehead to the sudden stiffness in his seated stance, she knew he deliberated his answer. She sensed his indecision.

"You might as well tell her the truth, Angus," Ned said from his position behind the bar. "Whether you like it or not, she's involved."

It looked to her as if it took a tremendous effort on his part to speak. Did he think her incapable of fitting into their little gathering of testosterone? Is that why he chose Colin over her in this matter, because he was a man?

Before she could stop herself, the words spilled out, "Is it because I'm a woman that you didn't include me in this?"

"Yes and no," he replied on a heavy breath. "Isabo, you have to understand that it wasn't me who laid down the guidelines of the society. It was set in place by the men of the clans, over two hundred years ago, that hid the MacKinnon brothers after the curse was placed upon them."

He paused, took a deep breath then continued. "Those men gave their oath to the sister of the MacKinnon brothers to protect the statues until a spell was found that could end the curse. This oath was handed down from generation to generation of fathers to sons. Only certain men of each clan were given this responsibility, never the women."

"So you chose Colin over me?"

"You see, lass," Ned intervened. "It wasn't your father's choice to keep you out of the society. If it was up to him, you would've been included long ago."

Izzy sat straight. She couldn't believe what she was hearing. But she should have known. This village was small and high in the Grampian Mountain region, where myths and legends ran deep. Many of the elders still believed in spirits roaming the earth. But her father? How could he have let the regiments of a time long gone rule his decisions, especially when it came to his only child, her? Heat slithered through her veins. Every muscle in her back tightened.

It was a male thing, the voice inside her brain whispered.

Instead of lashing out at the men in her life, she gritted her teeth and tried desperately to maintain a clear line of thought. There was something larger at stake here than the fact that she was excluded because she was a woman.

"To think that in today's time, male chauvinism still runs deep in our village," she spoke, keeping her voice as calm as possible while biting back her anger.

There was no changing what had happened, but she intended to let them know just how much they hurt her by not trusting her to uphold the oath of their forefathers simply because of her gender. She shot a sideways glance at Colin and caught him moving behind the bar, attempting to duck from her line of sight.

Good, let him stew on that for a while, she quipped to herself.

"There be that word again. Do all women of your world claim their men to suffer from this chauvinism?" A vaguely familiar male voice stated from near the front door, causing Izzy to spin around on her stool. Where had she heard that deep Scottish brogue before?

Oh, my God!

She blinked and her jaw dropped open. There was a living, breathing copy of the statue standing in the doorway. Granted, his features and his physique were so similar that he could have been the model from which the statue was carved, but Izzy doubted it.

Licking her suddenly dry lips, she closed her mouth and stood. The handsome hunk from the Internet Pub and plain-Jane entered. The woman audibly huffed as she moved forward. Her voice was soft as she spoke.

"Gavin, I've explained it to you before. I'm not going over it again. Not right now anyway."

"Hello, Gavin," Angus greeted as he stepped toward the man and shook his hand, then turned to the woman. "It's good to see you up and about, lassie."

"Morning, Angus," Gavin replied.

It surprised Izzy that he would even greet the man who she believed might have set fire to the cottage. She sprang at the man and shook her finger in his face. "How dare you show up here after what you did! You set fire to my father's cottage, and if you're a monk, you sure don't act it. I thought monks were men of peace and goodness, not destroyers of property or having sex with women."

The other woman's gasp had Izzy looking her up and down until the man named Gavin stepped between them as if becoming a protective barrier for the other woman.

"I be no monk, and as for the other, that be of a private nature and is not your concern." The stern tone of his voice Izzy recognized as a warning, but chose not to back down. Instead, she held her back taut, her chin lifted and a hard gaze fixed on his face until the rumble of her dad's robust laugh washed over her. Turning on her heels, she was greeted by his grin.

"Isabo, you are mistaken," he stated as his hand cupped her chin. "This is Gavin MacKinnon, not the monk who rented the cottage. But I do thank you for looking out for your ole man's best interest."

His large hands gathered her by the shoulders and turned her to face Gavin as he introduced her. "Gavin MacKinnon, this is my daughter, Isabo."

"You be the lass from the pub." His eyebrow cocked as a sheepish grin crossed his face as he said. "It is an honor to meet the daughter of a fine man. Please accept my apologies for the disturbance I caused in your place. It was my fault."

He turned sideways and the woman eased from behind him as he continued. "This be my lady, Ericka Russell."

"It's nice to meet you, Isabo."

"Izzy, please. My friends just call me Izzy." She managed to state as the other woman shook her hand.

"You'll have to forgive Gavin. He's a little behind in the ways of the world," Ericka said. Her smile seemed to brighten when Ericka glanced up at him and Izzy noted the heated gaze he slipped her way. Man, she wished someone would look at her that way, like he was going to devour her sexually the moment they were alone.

"But he's not a bad guy," Ericka continued as she wound her arm into the crook of his, causing him to clasp her hand. "Were you able to replace the computer that was broken?"

"Aye, it should be here soon." Izzy managed to reply, but she couldn't keep from staring at the giant next to plain-Jane...Ericka, she had to mentally remind herself. The woman had a name.

Standing this close to him, he held her imagination captive. Could it be possible that the curse was true? Was he truly a MacKinnon? And if so, how had he been freed? His facial features were so similar to that of the statue downstairs that she couldn't pull her eyes away. Strong chin, masculine cheekbones, straight nose, gorgeous eyes and a mouth that was tempting to taste. But it wasn't his mouth she wanted to taste. It was the one cast in stone and hidden in the cellar.

Oh God, where had that thought come from, she silently asked as she forced her gaze away from Gavin. Was she that desperate that she was hungering for a stone statue instead of the real thing? Man, was she lame, Izzy chastised herself. It took a tremendous effort to keep from staring at him again. But she couldn't stop the next thought from streaming through her brain. Were their eye colors the same? In her dreams, her version of the man never moved and had colorless eyes. Was it the statue in the cellar that she dreamed of?

A knot formed in her gut. All these years, was it a statue that held her subconscious captive? The sound of Gavin's voice snapped her from her thoughts, but it was his words that caught her attention.

"We've come to ask you if we could search the tavern. Ericka deciphered one of the riddles in Akira's diary, and from the sound of it, he's located in a drinking establishment. Your establishment seems to be the most likely place that one of me *brathairs* would be hidden, seeing as he spent many a night here."

"Seems we all thought the same," Ned quipped.

"We've got news for you," Angus smiled and with a tilt of his head in her direction, he added. "Isabo found him."

* * * * *

Hours had passed since she led Gavin and Ericka to the spot where one of the brothers was hidden. After Ericka slid out of the hole and confirmed that it was a MacKinnon, the men gathered the equipment needed to dismantle the wall protecting the statue. In order to not raise suspicion, Angus opened with Willie manning the bar. Ericka went with Izzy to the Internet Pub. It was thought to be best if everything appeared as if it were a normal day.

The suspense gnawed at Izzy's gut. She wanted to be there, to help tear down the wall surrounding her statue. *Her statue!* It wasn't hers. She held no claim to it. Izzy paced the length of the front window, gathering coffee and ale orders and assisting customers with getting online. With each stupid question she was asked, her patience thinned. For the first time in as long as she could remember, computer technology didn't consume her thoughts. The possibility that a man was frozen in stone demanded her brain waves.

How much longer before they called and let them know that the wall was down? What was keeping them? She rolled her eyes to the heavens as she flounced onto a stool beside Ericka at the bar. The speed of her fingers on the laptop keys was impressive.

"I wonder if he removed that site, because I can't seem to find it." Ericka stated in an exasperated tone.

"He might have gotten enough applications and took it down to cover his tracks. Let's see if he ever responded to my e-mail." Izzy replied as she logged onto her own laptop, connected to the internet and entered her e-mail server.

This was just the distraction she needed, because if she had to answer one more uneducated computer question, she was going to commit murder. And that would be bad for business, Izzy admitted to herself. She sighed, dissatisfied with her own lack of patience. Never had she been so unwilling to help the computer illiterate as she was today. Teaching another the joys of computer skills usually made her heart soar and her brain hum. This current discontent at the pub had to be caused by the situation at her dad's tavern, the not knowing. Gavin had been adamant that the wall's destruction be done as carefully as possible. In no way was the statue to be damaged. This had to be the reason for the delay. They must be doing it plank by plank and brick by brick, Izzy reckoned with a disheartened huff.

She skimmed through the sea of messages sent by her computer buddies from university. The chatter seemed endless, until the one she sought appeared with a red exclamation mark next to it in her spam filter. Should she share this with her newfound friend, Ericka, or should she keep her mouth shut until she could investigate it further? According to the application, the leader of the group wanted anyone who claimed to have a magical talent. Black magic was preferred. Ericka had stated that she had seen that site and application at one time, but couldn't find it now.

The woman beside her believed that the curse was real and that Gavin was a MacKinnon. She even stated that the statue in the cellar was a MacKinnon as well. If that were true, would she share the secret to freeing him with her? Izzy shifted in her seat at the thought of her giant in stone being a real flesh 'n' blood man. Just thinking about the things she wanted to try if the man from her dreams were able to actually respond to her touch had her temperature rising and her thong uncomfortably moist.

Darting a nervous tongue across her lips, Izzy tried to remain focused and reined in her overactive libido. Was it necessary to gain the other woman's trust in order to learn the way to free her man? Free her man! Oh God, she was losing it. The statue was not her man.

He could be. The sound of her mother's voice rippled softly through her ears, making her shiver in her seat. Izzy glanced around looking for the source of the whisper, then realized that it seemed that no one heard it but her. Ericka continued to tap away on her keyboard and the closest customer was engrossed in an online game. Neither even looked her way.

Izzy darted another glance around her place, then returned her stare to the daunting e-mail response. If she needed Ericka to help free the MacKinnon brother, so be it. But catching the monk who burned her dad's cottage to the ground was her business. She decided to reply to the information that she'd been sent at a later time, when she was alone, so she tucked the response in a saved file on her system.

"Must not have gotten around to answering the applications," Izzy fibbed and hoped Ericka bought it.

"Probably off licking his wounds," Ericka stated bluntly.

"Wounds?"

Ericka bit her lower lip. She looked from her laptop to Izzy. It seemed as if she wasn't sure what she should say. After several seconds, Ericka cleared her throat, then stated. "He was in the cottage when it caught fire."

"How would you know?" Izzy's eyebrow arched as she stared directly at Ericka. The other woman seemed to fidget as if trying to decide how much Izzy should know. Izzy didn't give her the chance to think things through and plan her speech. "You were there, weren't you? Don't deny it. I saw you in the back of Ned's car that night coming from the direction of the fire."

"I was," Ericka stated. "As I told you earlier, Brother Leod has an evil soul and a deadly mission to accomplish in his search for that book of black magic spells."

She paused, then continued as if deciding it was best to just tell Izzy the truth. "He claimed to be a direct descendant from Hume MacGillivray, the man who cursed the male heirs of the MacKinnon clan. The fire was an accident caused by his failed attempt to kill Gavin, using me as bait."

"What do you mean by bait?" Though she tried to refrain, Izzy couldn't hide the skepticism in her voice. The whole idea that a rogue monk was out to destroy the MacKinnon brothers' statues in a vain attempt to fulfill some obscure dark prophecy and lay claim to a black magic book was a bit too farfetched, *if* you asked her. But that's what Ericka and Gavin believed. Now Ericka was throwing in a part to the story about this so-called monk trying to kill Gavin and using her to get to him.

"I don't think it's missed your attention that Gavin and I are a pair." Ericka stopped fidgeting, sat straight and stared directly into Izzy's eyes. The intensity of her stare had Izzy stiffening her spine and swallowing hard. She hadn't meant to offend her newly acquired ally in this strange situation, but she knew from the look on Ericka's face that she had.

"I…" She didn't get to finish as Ericka cut her off with a raise of her hand in a stop motion.

Ericka smiled then stated,"I understand your reaction. I was completely caught off guard that a man as gorgeous as Gavin would be interested in a woman like me. I admit that I'm not the most beautiful woman out there. But he makes me feel like I am. I couldn't be happier or more in love as I am with him."

"I didn't mean to imply that there was something wrong with it." Izzy stuttered over her words, backtracking, trying to smooth over her mistake. "I'm sorry."

"Don't be. Fate handed me the man of my dreams, just as it has handed you yours."

"What?"

"Oh, Izzy." Ericka laughed a little as she spoke. "I saw the way you looked at Gavin when we arrived. It was as if you'd seen a ghost. Your eyes were dreamy and lust-filled, if I do say so myself."

"They were not," Izzy snapped as heat filled her cheeks.

"They were too," Ericka said with a smile. "It's the same way I look at him. And I know it's the same way you looked at the statue in the cellar. I saw it and I can tell you've been a bit defensive and edgy about its safety the whole time we've been down here waiting."

Before Izzy could think of a reply, Ericka continued. "I have to tell you, all of the brothers look similar in their features. But Gavin..." She paused on a heavy sigh, then continued. "He's the oldest. Ian, the one you found, is the second brother and if you saw him standing next to Gavin in the tapestry, you'd think they were twins at first glance. Only Ian's a hair shorter. The tapestry is a beautiful family portrait. You'll have to come out to the castle and see it for yourself. All seven of the MacKinnon boys as they were before they were cursed."

"This whole thing has me confused. Men turned to stone by a curse. Curses aren't real. Men don't turn to stone. It just doesn't happen." Izzy babbled in a low tone, hoping no one heard, because if they did, she was certain she'd be locked away in an asylum without a chance of release.

Ericka took Izzy's hand in hers and forced her to focus on her gaze. Her voice was soothing as she spoke. "Believe me. A few days ago, I was in the same state of mind as you. All my life, I never believed in anything that I could not prove with research and facts to base it on. But now it's my reality, as it is yours. You found him. I believe it's your destiny to release him from this curse."

Izzy saw in Ericka's eyes that she truly believed the words she had spoken. This woman wasn't some uneducated, backwoods being who lived and breathed in old world beliefs. Ericka was the same as she, multiple degreed, educated in the best of schools and extremely computer savvy.

And yet, here she sat, telling Izzy that fate had handed her the man of her dreams in the form of a statue created by a curse. Damn, what was she to believe? If her libido had its way, she'd fall for this line of fairy-tale rubbish, but her intellect tried desperately to cling to the last shred of sanity left in her gray matter.

"If this curse is real, prove it." Izzy stated point-blank as she tugged her hand free, sat straight and crossed her arms over her chest with her gaze leveled on Ericka's. "How did you free Gavin from his so-called prison of stone?"

"I knew you would ask that."

Ericka slid from the stool, walked around the bar to the printer and lifted a sheet of paper from its tray. As she handed it to Izzy, she said, "I printed a copy of the anti-curse for you. The words must be spoken as they are written, in Gaelic, and pronounced precisely in order for it to work."

"But I don't speak Gaelic," Izzy managed to mumble as she tried to fathom all the information thrust her way. Staring her in the face was proof, but was it real. If she spoke these words, would the statue turn to flesh?

"Neither did I. But I got a little help from a friend and now I'll help you." Ericka plopped back on the stool as she spoke. "That is, if you're willing to give it a try."

Izzy wasn't sure why she said it, but her mouth moved and the words escaped before she thought better of them.

"I am."

Chapter Seven

ॐ

By dinner time, Izzy's patience was depleted. She spent the majority of her afternoon attempting to learn an ancient Gaelic passage with the diligent taskmaster Ericka as her speech instructor. Imagine that, she griped silently, a Yankee teaching a Scot the proper pronunciation of Gaelic. Her mother would never have let her live that one down if she were still alive. The sound of her mother's voice speaking the ancient tongue to her when she was a little girl echoed in her memory. How she wished now that she'd paid more attention then.

She closed the Internet Pub, gathered her laptop and convinced Ericka that they should check in with the men. The lack of communication from them had not only Izzy on edge, but she sensed Ericka wasn't as relaxed as she attempted to portray. Something must have gone wrong and no one thought to tell them. The sun was low in the sky as she and Ericka walked down the street toward the tavern.

Several of the regulars were there when they entered. Willy was behind the bar with two men seated across from him. None of the others were visible, which led Izzy to believe they were still in the cellar.

Common courtesy had Izzy stopping and speaking to a few of the older men gathered at the single occupied table in the tavern. They were there every day. It amazed her that they seemed to have nothing else to do other than drink, eat and play cards.

One glance in Willy's direction and she received a subtle nod toward the office. She acknowledged it with a polite nod of her own and excused herself and Ericka from the men. It was all she could do not to run toward the closed door.

She tapped once, then opened the door, slipped inside with Ericka close on her heels and shut it behind them. No one was in the room, but she knew why. The large antique liquor cabinet was moved and now sat several feet to the right of its normal position. A trapdoor was open in the floor.

Izzy placed her laptop on the desk and walked over to the opening. Light illuminated up through the hole. The low mumble of male voices echoed as she carefully eased onto the ladder that leaned against the wall of the cellar. With each step, she noticed the rickety wooden ladder from her dream was actually built into the wall, behind the metal one she was now climbing down on.

Caught up in the memory of that ladder breaking with her on it in her dream, she hesitated. Warm strong hands clasped her waist from behind, startling her into motion.

"Here, lassie." Gavin's deep Scottish brogue rolled over her, sending a wave of chills to her skin and a hint of heat to her cheeks. "Let me help you down."

"Thank you," she managed to whisper when her feet touched the ground. But his hands were already off her the moment she was settled and he was reaching for Ericka. With her, Izzy noticed him linger. It was as if he didn't want to let her go, but did so with great effort.

Would his brother be that gentle in his touch? Would his hands not want to leave her body like Gavin's seemed to not want to leave Ericka's? Izzy swallowed hard and forced her feet to function. She spun around and headed straight to the area where the others still worked.

"Izzy, child, what time is it?" Her dad sputtered as he straightened, lowering the spade he held in his hand.

"It's close to five o'clock," Izzy stated as she inspected the wall. "What's taking so long to bring down a wall?"

Many of the bricks lining the wall were shattered, or removed and lay in a pile off to the side. Thick beams stood coated in what looked to be a mixture of dried mud and horse hair. The original hole was now large enough for a man Gavin's size to crawl through, but not much bigger than that. A strange array of knotted rope and rusted thin sheaths of wire were intermixed in the partially dismantled section of wall above the hole.

Colin pointed to the ropes and wires as he spoke. "Seems the forefathers planted a trap. From what we've gathered so far, these are connected to several of the beams in the ceiling above the statue and in the floorboards above our heads. If they vibrate too much, the floor above us shakes and the area above him starts dumping dirt in on him."

"What?" she gasped. Izzy knelt to look through the hole and saw a layer of dirt coating Ian's statue. A knot tightened in her gut. If the ceiling caved, would he survive? Would his statue crumble?

"Don't you worry none, lass," Ned stated as he surprised her by bending over so she could see him standing on the other side. His dirty face beamed a bright smile her way. "I've added support to this side and shored up the ceiling above him. We just have to be careful not to bang too hard or jar the boards I put up."

"Can't you just cut the ropes and wires?" Izzy suggested in a form of a question.

"No," her dad said, shaking his head. "We tried that with the first one we came across. That's how we learned what they were for."

"Yeah," Colin added. "The whole room rumbled and a cloud of dust shot out of the hole when one of the beams above his head shifted. It's some sort of geared contraption held in place by the tautness of the lines. We can't even tug on them or the beams shift, dumping crap in on us."

"We're having to dig Ian out layer by layer."

Izzy turned to look at Gavin. The sadness in his voice was mirrored in his face. It had to be tough for him to be this close, yet still so far from achieving the goal of unlocking his brother from his prison.

God, was she believing this? Izzy dragged her gaze from Gavin's face and turned to stare at the hole. Was that truly a man entombed on the other side of that wall? If the raw emotion she swore she saw on Gavin's face was any implication, then this wasn't a myth…this was fact.

"Hey, down there," Willy called down into the cellar. "Margaret and Ms. May are here with food."

"We don't want to be raising suspicions," Ned said as he came through the hole in the wall. "Can't be sure who's there."

"I'll head up through the bar and I'll let you know." Colin stated as he dusted himself off, then walked over to the wall that turned and pushed it open farther until he squeezed through.

After a few minutes, he poked his head through the opening. "Coast is clear. Margaret ran the men playing cards home to their wives. You're free to come up."

Ned and Angus followed Colin through the turning wall. Ericka nudged Gavin toward the opening. "You need to eat. You won't be of any use if you're too weak to help move him out of there when the time comes."

Out of the corner of her eye, Izzy saw the gentle giant place a kiss to Ericka's forehead before he wiggled through the opening and extended his hand to her. "You comin', milady?"

"In a minute," she replied. "You go on ahead. I'll be right there."

Even though the enticing scent of Margaret's cooking drifted down the stairs, Izzy wasn't hungry. She didn't want to leave him alone in the cellar. The wall looked shaky and weakened by the removal of much of the brick and mortar that held it in place. A gentle touch to her elbow caused Izzy to look from the wall to the woman beside her. Ericka leaned in close and whispered.

"I think you know what needs to be done." With that said, Ericka turned and exited through the rotated wall.

Izzy was dumbfounded. The woman couldn't possibly think that she...on reflex her hand slid into the leather pouch attached by a strap hung low around her hips. Trembling fingers withdrew the piece of paper with the anti-curse on it that she had practiced speaking for most of the afternoon. This was crazy, she sighed.

What do you have to lose, the inner voice whispered. Nothing, she decided as she held the paper tight and crawled through the hole into the statue's chamber.

Every muscle tightened as she straightened. The room had changed since her last visit. It seemed smaller due to the planks of wood that were installed along the walls and ceiling for added support. Her hand shook as she brushed the dirt that had fallen from his eyes and face. Licking her lips, she swallowed hard, trying to muster enough moisture in her mouth to speak the words. She stepped back, raised the paper to eye level, cleared her throat then spoke.

"Ceum saor de clach.

Be ye biast air duine.

'Tis gaol dara slighe.

Ge ye be meinne,

dh' oidhche mur,

dh' la."

"Step free of stone, be ye beast or man, 'tis love either way, though ye be mine by night, if not by day." Izzy repeated the phrase in its translated form as if hearing what it meant would add validity to the situation.

"Nice try, my daughter."

An icy chill filled the air as Izzy's mother appeared, hovering near the statue. Izzy froze, her eyes widened and her jaw dropped. This couldn't be happening again. Cold transparent fingers sent chills scurrying down her neck as they sent a sensation of touch to her cheek when her mother's ghostly hand brushed near her face.

"You must speak the words with feeling and mean the words you say."

The figure shaped like her mother floated to stand beside her. Its cold essence wrapped her in a chilling hug, but she wasn't afraid. Images of love and happiness filled her mind. Her mother's love warmed her soul, even though every inch of her skin was ice cold from the spirit's essence lingering around her.

"Think back to when you were little. Remember the story I told you of the young woman who found and freed her love from a world of solitary confinement."

Izzy simply nodded as she closed her mouth and stared at the image of her mother.

"That story was of you. This is your moment to shine. I found the parchment with the riddle of his location tucked away in the family bible while pregnant with you and knew it was a sign. I searched for him until I found what I thought to be a hidden room in the cellar. But I never found the entrance. You found it as a child. It's time for you to remember, Izzy."

The brightness of her mother's smile forced Izzy's lips to curl into a timid smile as she watched the transparent image. Did she believe her eyes? Was this truly her mother visiting her? The sensation of touch graced her brow as her mother's hand came near her face. Inside her head, it seemed as if a veil lifted and a hidden memory surfaced as her mother spoke.

"Remember back to a warm afternoon when you and Colin were playing in the bar. You hid in your favorite place, the bottom of the cabinet in your father's office. Instead of lying still, you found a latch, tugged on it until it gave way and you climbed through the hatch to the hidden cellar room. I watched over you as you discovered the statue. You weren't scared. It made me proud when you left Melinda to keep him company. I knew that if you told your father, he would try to free him before it was time. After you climbed back up, I gave you the strength to close the hatch and lock it, then I sheltered the memory from you. Please forgive me. It had to be done to keep him safe."

A devilish gleam shone in her mother's eyes. When she shot a wink at her, Izzy swallowed the urge to laugh. She remembered that look. The mischievous nature that ran through her veins was a gift from her mother's genes and she knew it. That fact was reiterated by her dad every time she'd gotten into trouble.

"In all my searches, I never discovered the opening, but you did. I knew in my heart that when the time was right, you would find him again. This MacKinnon brother was meant for you. He is your soul mate trapped within that stone. Now say those words with feeling and mean it."

A gentle wind against her back acted as a shove, causing Izzy to step forward. Glancing across her shoulder, she saw the image of her mother dissipate, leaving her to stand alone. Lifting her shoulders, straightening her back and tilting her chin, Izzy mustered every ounce of feeling she could draw from the images her mother stirred to life in her head.

Love, happiness and the unity of family flowed in her voice as she spoke the words in perfect Gaelic.

"Ceum saor de clach.

Be ye biast air duine.

'Tis gaol dara slighe.

Ge ye be meinne,

dh' oidhche mur,

dh' la."

Outside, the early shadows of evening had fallen. The ground under her feet rumbled, startling Izzy, causing her to stumble backward. Dust filled the air, making her squint, but the sight before her she refused to miss. She couldn't pull her eyes away even if she wanted too. Bit by bit, stone crumbled from the statue to pool around its feet. She coughed and gagged with each breath she took and still she forced herself to remain where she stood. Minutes seemed like hours as the dust settled and her vision cleared.

Oh, my God, it looked as if the myth was real. A gorgeous hunk of Scottish warrior stood living and breathing within a few feet of her and all she could do was stare.

Situated in a battle ready stance, the man Gavin called Ian looked directly at her. The deepest blue eyes she had ever seen seemed to penetrate straight through her, sending signals of raw need to her pussy. If it wasn't for the support of the wall behind her, she was certain that her knees would have given way under the weight of his stare. Within seconds, the tip of his sword hovered beneath her chin, pointed at the rapid throb of the pulse in her neck.

Was he kidding? Did he actually mean to kill her after she had set him free?

Afraid to even swallow due to the close proximity of the sword's tip to her skin, Izzy stood still. But she couldn't determine whether it was fear or sexual adrenaline that made her inner muscles clench and her legs quiver. This was stupid. What was she supposed to do now? Unable to resist, she let her gaze slide down the man.

Even though he was hunched in a battle stance, she knew he was tall, much taller than she. He had to be no less than six feet. A broad chest rippled with muscles. His biceps flexed as his hand tightened on the sword's hilt. Pure strength seemed to ooze out of him and she was impressed that he held such a large and heavy looking sword extended and unwavering in one hand. Naked from the waist up, she couldn't help but notice the cut texture of his abdominal muscles. Her nipples pebbled at the thought of skin-to-skin contact with those washboard abs.

Unable to look any lower due to the position of his sword, she lifted her gaze back to his face. Those brilliant blue eyes darted from side to side as if trying to determine his location.

His face was taut and confusion was evident. But what did she expect?

He was scared.

* * * * *

What form of sorcery was this? Ian shook, sending remnants of stone and dirt to the floor while holding his sword ready to attack his enemy. He knew not where he was, no matter which direction he looked. The room was small with only one other near. But what was it? Was it human?

Wide-eyed, he stared at the creature standing at the end of his drawn sword. Dressed in black, it stood, not flinching or moving, but staring back at him with big green eyes outlined in thick black war paint. Bright red lips made him think of blood. But whose blood did this creature drink to achieve such a color?

He took a deep breath and steadied his stance. Short white spikes stood on its head where hair should be. Or was that its hair? He couldn't be sure. Never had he seen such a color. A strange restraint made of leather and decorated with some sort of metal studs was around its neck. Was it a slave? Glancing down its body, he realized the creature was a woman. The sight of its chest heaving, lifting round globes with each breath, caused an unwanted reaction beneath his kilt.

Nay, 'tis not the time for this, he silently chided his growing member as he forced his gaze lower and away from his favorite female part. But that was a mistake. The woman wore a black skirt of indecent length. Any shorter and her nether region would be exposed for all to see. As it was, the woman had outstanding legs. Milky white thighs made him lick his lips. Her calves and feet were hidden, encased in some sort of black leather boots. He envisioned himself nestled in a gripping hug with those legs wrapped around his waist and her leather-clad ankles locked at the small of his back.

Ian swallowed hard and tried to focus on anything other than the strange female creature. But it was difficult, considering the room was small and there was nothing more enticing to look at other than her odd, yet appealing, features. Even though her appearance was the strangest he had ever seen, he decided she was dressed for sex.

If he lifted her skirt, would she be naked, wet and ready for him?

Och, what was wrong with him? Ian stiffened. Darting his gaze from side to side, he tried desperately to determine where he was being held prisoner. Anything to not look at the enticing creature locked in this small room with him. Maybe she would know the answer if he asked.

"*Càite 'tis seo àite?*"

She did not understand the words that left his lips. Izzy gathered her strength and forced her hand to lift. From the look on his face, she knew it surprised him when she clasped the end of his sword carefully between her fingers and thumb and stepped sideways away from its tip. He sprang back, still holding his sword directed at her while sputtering another word in Gaelic that she didn't understand.

"*Stad!*"

"Oh, cut it out," she snapped at him. The look on his face would have had her laughing in a normal situation, but this wasn't normal.

Before she could do anything else, Gavin worked his way thorough the hole and rolled in one move into a standing position between her and the end of his brother's sword. With space in the room being limited, she was scrunched between Gavin's back and the wall.

"Ian, my *brathair. Yer an saor.*"

Gavin's arms extended. Ian's sword lowered and they stepped together in a brotherly hug. The two chatted in rapid Gaelic for several seconds, as if forgetting she existed, until she nudged Gavin in the small of his back.

"Ah, milady," Gavin said as he turned slightly to let her out from behind him. "Please forgive me." He took her hand as if presenting her to his brother and added, "My *brathair*, this is Isabo MacDonell, the lady who freed you."

Izzy noted the slight nod of Ian's head as his gaze scrutinized her from head to toe. Her nipples tingled when his eyes lingered at her chest. Clearing her throat, Izzy said, "I understand your excitement. But don't you think it would be better for all concerned, if we get him out of here."

As if to emphasize her statement, a cloud of dust and dirt filtered through the support boards above their heads.

"Aye, you lead the way," Gavin replied.

She didn't need to be asked twice. Izzy scooted to the hole and crawled in. Today had definitely taking a turn for the strange. A visit from her mother compiled with an ancient Scottish laird breaking free from a statue right in front of her eyes topped the list at number one strange day. She glanced across her shoulder and noticed that Ian's deep blue gaze was locked on her bottom. An unstoppable smile stretched her lips. She knew the length of her skirt in this position gave him a peek at her arse, not to mention her thong.

Instant heat pooled in between her lower lips, sending shivers up her abdomen. Damn, she was hot for him and he hadn't even touched her. It had to be the shade of his eyes, she decided. His eyes were more beautiful than she could ever have imagined in any of her dreams.

But could she make him hers? In her dreams, he never returned her affections. That little smidgeon of doubt made her gut knot as she stood on the other side of the hole. What would it take to make him look at her the way Gavin looked at Ericka?

God, she wished she knew.

Chapter Eight

ɞ

He counted ten new recruits. He sighed as he skimmed the new set of files he retrieved from his site. Each one he had responded to earlier in the day, just before removing his presence from the internet. It would not pay to have one of the monks devout in the old ways of the brotherhood stumble upon his intent to build a following with those dedicated to the art of black magic. Once his membership was strong, he planned to take over the monastery founded by his ancestor, Hume MacGillivray, and turn it into what he felt it was meant to be…a brotherhood of the dark arts.

In his mind, the doctrine was clear. Its passages were written by a MacGillivray for a direct descendent of their clan to become master of the book. His interpretation led him to believe that he, Hume Leod MacGillivray, was that descendent. Even though his first attempt to follow the rules of the prophecy and rid the world of the MacKinnon scum failed, it was a temporary setback. He knew the book was protected by a spell that would not break until the prophecy had been fulfilled. It was his destiny to complete the task of the prophecy, which was to rid the world of the seven MacKinnon brothers.

Several centuries prior, Hume MacGillivray used a curse from the Book of Shadows to turn the brothers to stone. Each were hidden by their sister, Akira, to protect them from destruction before the Brotherhood of Our Sons of the Servant of Justice could find them and complete the purification as demanded by Hume. The hunt was relinquished many years ago and the monastery turned into a sanctuary for the book, keeping it safe from those who would use it for their advantage. The book was evil. Leod hungered for control over this ancient art of sorcery. With it, he planned to rule his newfound brotherhood of black magic souls.

Among these ten new applicants, he hoped to find at least one or two with a power he could manipulate. The others were probably Goth wannabes or magicians with weak tricks who yearned for the knowledge of real dark magic. He snickered, then stopped and sat upright.

The cursor on his screen blinked beside the name and a postal box on one of the information forms.

It was a female named Inez. The postal box gave no clues to an exact home address, but the town was familiar. Had he missed something when he was there? Was this Inez the Gothic chick from the Internet Pub? No, he sighed. If he remembered correctly, her name was Izzy, not Inez. Heat filled his soul at the thought of the first woman to answer his internet call. He could only hope she was as hot as that Gothic chick Water rolled down his cheek from his injured eye as he squinted to reread the name. No, he shook his head. It read Inez, not Izzy.

If he had met this Inez when he was there, he could have used this woman to his advantage. Maybe taken the edge off his need, sated his sexual desires or at least slackened them a bit before he tackled the MacKinnon and his woman. Leod's jaw tightened as his mistake resurfaced in his thoughts. He'd let his dick think too much for him in the case of that one named Ericka. He'd let the knowledge that she belonged to a MacKinnon rule his thoughts until he was blind with fury.

That anger fueled his need to plow his cock into her and show her what it was like to be fucked by a real man. A man who would one day command the power of the Book of Shadows, the book filled with the knowledge of the world's darkest magic and incantations. And he would be its ruler. On that day, he would show Ericka what it felt like to have a man of power between her thighs. She would pay for being the demise of his plan to rid the world of one of the MacKinnon clan. Gavin MacKinnon was marked for death, as were all of the MacKinnon brothers, of that he was sure.

He stared at the contact information. This one was female enough to staunch his sexual needs. Should he drop this recruit another e-mail or wait?

Though it took a great effort to control the pain stemming from his freshly set shoulder, he reached between his legs and fondled his naked balls. With his other hand, he typed another note to the woman, reiterating the need for them to meet. A tap of the send button and he knew it was simply a matter of time before she would reply. Until then…Leod shoved back from the computer desk, replaced his left arm in its sling, leaned back in the leather swivel chair and caressed his semi-swollen cock with his good hand.

The woman's e-mail had him picturing the Gothic chick in his head. Maybe they were sisters, He sighed. Izzy's features filtered through his thoughts as his grip tightened on his shaft. Spiked white hair, dark-lined eye makeup, bright red lips and a decent set of breasts, if his memory of the girl were correct, she would suit his needs and relieve his frustration quite nicely.

Uhm, the things he'd have her do with those bright red lips. Thinking of the places on his body he'd have her suck made his gut clench at the idea. Pre-cum oozed out of the tip of his cock and he spread it on the head until it glistened. Picturing her head bobbing in his hands while consuming his dick made his pace quicken as his fingers wound around his shaft, rubbing up and down, harder and harder until he arched, lifting his bottom from the seat. Back flat against the chair, feet planted on the floor, thighs spread wide, he grabbed his balls, massaging the taut sac, then fisted his cock until his cum spewed onto his abdomen.

Cum continued to seep from his cock as unwanted visions of Ericka and Gavin burned behind his closed lids. Leod shot upright, gasping for air. Those two had to die and soon. Just thinking about them revived the pain of his burned and tortured flesh, causing him to scream.

The dislocated shoulder gave him limited pain due to the fact it was a common occurrence for him since childhood. But the burns were different. These were gifted to him by the hand of his enemy. Each streak of pain through his system intensified his hatred for the MacKinnons. Try as he might, no amount of magic energy from within his soul contained his pain or rid it from his flesh. Magic did not relinquish his suffering. Instead he was forced to turn to the medicines of man.

"Doc!" His scream echoed out of his bedroom and down the hall.

The sound of running footsteps greeted his ears and stopped when they reached his side. Only then did he attempt to open his eyes again. Two men stood beside him. One he had known since they were children and knew he was easily manipulated. The other he had lured into his web of deceit and lies with the promise of wealth, power and money. More money than any London doctor would ever make in a lifetime. Though this man's mind was strong, there were moments of weakness and at those times he was Leod's to control. Knowing the Doc's darkest secrets gave Leod the factors needed to manipulate him without magic.

"Leod, what are you doing out of bed?" Doc sputtered as he spoke, while fumbling with his wire-rimmed, thick-lensed glasses. The short skinny man looked disheveled standing in a dingy white t-shirt and a pair of dark sweatpants.

Leod couldn't help but notice Doc's steady stare at his cock and the nervous dart of his tongue across his bottom lip. The man's true weakness was obvious. A twisted smile tugged at Leod's lips as he teased.

"Couldn't avoid a bout of internet porn."

As Leod caressed his cock, Doc's eyes widened and his voice shook as he spoke. "You should rest. I'll get my bag and give you another dose of pain meds."

Doc turned on his heels and hurried from the room. A low laugh rumbled from Leod's throat until a cloth landed on his belly. Leod's gaze snapped from the doorway to the face of the other man in the room.

"You should not tease 'im like that. You know how 'e is." The large man spoke in a rapid Scottish accent. Redheaded and barrel-chested, Roy Finnegan was a loyal minion, built like a pit bull dog and just as mean and ugly.

"Aye," Leod replied with a snort as he wiped the semen from his abdomen, then tossed the cloth on the floor. "I know what he likes. Jealous, Roy?"

Leod arched his brow and puckered his lips in a teasing kiss. Roy snorted as he stated, "You know the only meat I eats is pussy. Now let me help you back to bed before Doc returns and offers you more than a helping hand and a needle prick."

Within seconds of Leod returning to bed, Doc entered with a black medical bag in hand. Leod shook his head when Roy lifted the edge of the blanket and started to pull it up from the foot of the bed. Roy huffed and left the room, shaking his head. But Leod knew that keeping the Doc entertained was the main objective. If the man's sexual interest was piqued, then he was bound and determined to please the object of his desires. At the moment, Leod didn't care that it was he the Doc wanted.

Odd, the Doc's interest didn't bother him, Leod surmised as he watched the Doc fumble with his bag, gathering a syringe, a needle and a small bottle of pain medication. Sprawled naked on a bed in front of a man he knew had a lurid past due to his inability to keep his hands off the private parts of his former male patients should upset him, or in the least repulse him. Instead, he found it rather invigorating.

"Roll on to your hip, please."

The Doc's soft-spoken words lured him from his thoughts. Though the man held a medicine filled syringe in one hand and a cotton ball coated with alcohol in the other, Leod noted the man's gaze was firmly planted on his cock. Not ready to spoil the fun he was having at the Doc's expense, he grabbed his limp shaft and in a slow, deliberate motion, stroked it. He heard the audible hitch in the other man's throat and saw the dilation of his pupils and the subtle flare of his nostrils. Watching the Doc's reaction was entertaining, but the sizzle of pain down the side of his face and neck reminded him of the need for what was in that syringe. Without releasing his cock, Leod turned up on his hip, away from the Doc.

The sting of the sharp jab was nothing compared to the immediate burn of the morphine entering his system. Warmth cocooned his deviant soul, soothing his pain as he lay on his back and nestled his head against the pillow. His eyelids grew heavy and the game for him was over. The soft sensation of his hand being lifted from his cock and placed beside his thigh sent a warning that his limbs were incapable of reacting to.

Tender motions caressed his balls and trailed the length of his flaccid cock as the whispered words reached his ears. "Too bad the morphine makes you unable to get hard."

A heated tongue licked from his ball sac to the tip of his cock, tickling the slender opening before he felt the covers slide up over him. If he were able, would he have let the Doc blow him? What difference was one mouth from another? *May have to try that, if the woman isn't compliant*, he reasoned in his drug-induced haze before succumbing to sleep.

* * * * *

Izzy met Ericka, Ned, her dad and Colin on the other side of the wall. Before she could explain what had happened, Gavin came through the wall first, followed by Ian. When he stood to full height, Izzy's breath caught in her throat. He stood at over six foot, but just a hair shorter than Gavin. Ian rolled his head from side to side, stretching his neck, while at the same time lifting his shoulders and pressing them back, as if trying to ease the tightness being captured in stone for over two hundred years caused. His shoulders flexed back increased the broad expanse of his chest, making Izzy ache to snuggle against him and cuddle in his strength.

"It's so good to meet you, Ian," Ericka said as she extended her hand and he took it.

A sudden pang of jealousy knotted Izzy's gut. Ericka had a man of her own, why touch hers? Izzy shot her gaze to the floor and tried desperately to control these unfamiliar sensations pinging through her system. What claim did she have to him? She may have stated the words, but did that mean that he was hers?

As Gavin got involved with the conversation, he introduced his brother to the others in the cellar using both English and Gaelic. Only half listening, she heard Gavin explaining the situation in a mixture of both languages, causing her to understand a word here and there.

Her eyes had a mind of their own and refused to remain off Ian's form.

Every visible inch of him hinted of his masculinity. Her throat dried as her gaze soaked in his massive build. No man she had ever met looked this good to her, not even Gavin. Well, maybe Gavin, but he was taken.

His wide-legged stance enhanced the size of his legs. From what she could see, one of his thick muscled thighs was more than twice the size of hers and his calves made hers look like toothpicks. But it was the impressive lump beneath his kilt that commanded her attention. Whether intentional or not, it moved in an up-and-down motion without the help of a hand. Damn, what muscle control the man had, shot through Izzy's thoughts as she forced her eyes up and met his heated gaze.

Hot, deep blue eyes stared directly at her. If she wasn't mistaken, she thought she saw a hint of mischief in his gaze. Was he intentionally teasing her? A quick glance around and she realized the others were leaving the cellar and had not noticed his trick. Were they expected to follow? If they lingered, would she get a peek beneath that kilt?

Izzy rolled her eyes upward, trying to think of things less desirable than him in order to gain control over her rampant libido. Turning on her heels, she forced her legs to move and headed toward the exit. A strong hand cupped her elbow, stopping her in her tracks. Warm lips nuzzled her ear lobe as he spoke.

"I owe you my life, milady," he whispered in a rough form of English as he shifted closer to her back. Pure heat caressed the tender skin of her neck as he continued. His voice, ragged and low, switched to Gaelic. "My *dona boireannach*, you have me *cruaidh 'n acras* for your sheath."

It didn't take an interpreter for her to understand his meaning the moment his rock-hard cock brushed her bottom in an upward caress. Even though they were clothed, its length and rigidity was distinguishable, sending sheer pangs of need to her clit which tightened and throbbed without being touched. How had he done that to her?

Before she could speak or think, the tip of his tongue traced her ear. One arm wrapped around her waist, tugging her tighter against his chest. The sensation of bare skin brushed her back and weakened her knees. If his arm wasn't holding her in a comfortable grip, she would have crumpled to the floor. Not given the chance to react, his other hand was beneath the short hem of her skirt before she could gather her senses. His finger wasted no time. It homed in on her pussy and slid between the moist lips, circled her aching nub before teasing her opening.

Every protest she knew she should be stating dissipated in her brain. Her inner muscles clenched, drawing his finger in deeper, coating it with a flood of her juices. This wasn't right. She knew she should stop him, but not one ounce of her wanted too. Behind her stood the man from her dreams. His arm was around her, holding her close, his mouth hovered near her ear, his heated breath caressed her skin and his finger teased her beyond belief.

If this was somehow a dream, she prayed she wouldn't wake up.

His other hand massaged its way up her abdomen, leaving a trail of goose bumps in its wake. Izzy's breath shifted to short and shallow in tune with the movement of his finger in and out of her slit. When his other finger and thumb maneuvered under the lacy cup of her bra and captured her ripe hard nipple, her heart skipped a beat and breathing was suspended. The way he rolled her sensitive tip between his fingers and gave it a series of tender tugs made her gasp for a much-needed breath. If he kept this up, she would orgasm at any second.

But he didn't.

To her disappointment, he let go of her breast, removed his finger as swiftly as he had entered and turned her around to face him, all in one smooth move. The sight of his chest heaving with deep breaths and his cock tenting his kilt let her know he was as excited as she. Why stop?

Movement above their heads echoed through the floorboards and they both looked up. They were expected upstairs. As it was, they had lingered a bit too long and if they were not careful, someone would come down to check and see what was keeping them.

In a bold movement, Izzy grabbed his head in her hands, tugged him downward, tiptoed and planted a full-lipped heated kiss on his mouth. Panic knotted her gut as visions of stone-cold kisses from her dreams entered her mind for a split second before he responded. A hot moist tongue speared her mouth, parting her lips and taking command of their kiss. Her back pressed against the wall, her arms wrapped around his neck as centuries of pent-up passion filtered through his kiss.

Capable hands lifted her from the floor and guided her legs around his waist. How he managed to move his kilt out of the way amazed her. The shortness of her skirt was no interference at all. With her legs hugging him, it gave him easy access to her sex. A soft moan echoed up her throat as the plump head of his cock teased her dripping slit. Tremors ran up and down her inner thighs. Need for him to fill her made her whole being ache and shiver, hovered on the edge of reaching her deepest desire…to finally have the man from her dreams. The one who haunted her every thought when it came to sex. Though she never realized it before now, he was the man she had waited for to have the ultimate orgasm.

But she would have to continue the wait. Gavin's voice echoed down the stairwell.

"Ian, you all right?"

Pure fire simmered in his hooded gaze as he stared into her eyes. Holding her gaze prisoner with his, he watched her reaction as he slid the full length of his rigid shaft up between her swollen lower lips, tapping her clit with the head. From his smile, she knew he liked her parted lipped gasp and the unstoppable widening of her eyes. But how could she react any other way? The man was a sexual master and, for some reason, he controlled her body without any form of restraint on her part. This wasn't like her. Usually, she held the reins of pleasure and guided her sex partner in the art of pleasing her. But not with Ian. He was in total control and it excited her beyond any experience she'd ever tried.

"Aye," Ian called to Gavin as he lowered her to her feet. The moment he was certain she was steady, he released her and straightened his kilt. "The lady and I shall be up in a moment."

A smile split her lips at his awkward attempt to hide his hard-on. A kilt wasn't the best clothing to accomplish that feat. In his case, she didn't think any form of clothing would hide his package, not in its hardened condition.

"You think this funny, do you?" Ian faced her with a broad smile and an arched brow above one eye. He grabbed her in a one-armed hug, cupped the back of her head in his

101

other hand and spoke in a hushed tone with his lips hovered within millimeters of hers.

"Your scent coats my cock, my *dona leannan*. It is a scent which has me hungry for more than just a tease in the ale cellar. You shall have me balls deep in your sheath this night, my *dona* Isabo. This be a promise I shall keep."

Ian's kiss was rough, commanding, yet passionate and hinted of sexual fantasies he was determined to fulfill. It was all Izzy could do to stay standing when he released her. Never had a man spoken to her as blatantly as he had and gotten away with it, much less turned her on. Even the sound of her given name on his lips increased the heat burning in her blood. And by God, she was hot. Turned on didn't come close to expressing how she was at that instant. Nothing she'd tried before compared to the sensation of tremendous need pooling in her pussy caused by Ian's raw sexual desire.

Unable to do anything more, Izzy nodded in compliance, turned and forced her legs to work and led him through the opened wall to the stairs. She sensed him directly behind her on the stairs. Before they reached the top, he clasped her hips, stopped her for a second, nudged his head under her short skirt and marked her bottom with his teeth. Pain and ecstasy shot through her system. Liquid flooded between her lower lips and she hoped that it didn't stream down her inner thighs. Across her shoulder, she met his gaze as he let go of her hips.

"You are mine this night. Don't you forget it."

Izzy opened her mouth, then closed it. This man was going to be the death of her, but what a way to go. Before he could torment her any more, she scooted up the stairs and into the bar. Stepping out of the stairwell and up onto the floor, she stood, straightened her skirt and top and tried to regain her composure.

The taste of her lips lingered on his tongue, increasing his hunger for the woman. Her scent filled each breath, making it more difficult to abate his hard-on. If his brother had not interfered, she would have been up against the wall with his shaft sheathed within her warmth. Lifting his fingers to his nose, her musky smell of arousal coated his skin. She was ready and willing to be his *dona leannan*.

If his *brathair* was right, he had been imprisoned in stone for more than two hundred years. A wicked smile split his lips. That was a long time to be without a woman. No wonder his shaft was hard. The bounce of her short skirt as she climbed the stairs in front of him added to his interest.

Did all women of this time wear such? If so, being cursed for so many years was to his favor. In his time, long skirts and thick blouses hid their treasures. Watching Izzy's lush bottom sway was a pleasure he would not soon forget. Her flesh had reddened from the nip of his teeth, marking her as his for the night. Many others had received his mark and worn it as a badge of honor among the *dona boireannachs* of the villages and surrounding lands. Would the women of this time be as willing to seek their pleasures with a *brathair* of the MacKinnon clan?

At the top of the stairs, Izzy's position gave him full view up her skirt. The thin garment she wore did nothing but part her lower lips, making them seem as if they were pouting and waiting for his kiss. Ian's cock twitched and he stopped for a moment to gather his strength. It wouldn't do to enter the unknown as randy as a young man on his first romp with a woman.

Nay, he sighed. He needed control over his shaft. Think of the ugliest beast of the woods. Though he tried, visions of Izzy's luscious pussy burned behind his closed lids. What he needed was a romp with the odd-looking beauty. Short white hair, dark-lined eyes, bright red lips, round full breasts, milk-white long legs and a sheath moist and ready for his shaft, no matter how different her looks were from the women he had known, she still held his interest beyond belief.

Aye, he decided, he'd seek his pleasure with Izzy this night. And if the condition of his shaft were any proof, he'd seek it more than once.

* * * * *

The tavern was empty except for their group. Her dad hung a sign in the window stating that they were temporarily closed for a private party. Izzy knew everyone with the exception of one woman. She stood even with Ericka in height, and had shoulder-length hair, which was a vibrant, red shade with faint streaks of gray around the temples. The flowing silk kimono-styled robe she wore reminded Izzy of the sort a china doll would wear, except the colors were too wild in its shades of green, yellow and orange. A pair of matching slippers peeked from under the hem. Each move the woman made was echoed by the sound of the many different bracelets around her wrists. Long dangling earrings sporting what Izzy assumed were rubies, emeralds and diamonds glittered in the light and her fingers were covered in matching rings. If Izzy thought her style was over the top, Goth had nothing on this woman.

"Izzy, I'd like you to meet my Aunt May," Ericka said as she guided the other woman toward Izzy.

Sensing Ian coming out of the stairwell, Izzy stepped around the end of the bar to greet the woman. To keep her composure, she needed space between herself and Ian, even though with each movement she was reminded of how wet she was for him.

"It's nice to meet you."

"Likewise…" May's voice faltered as she moved past Izzy toward the hulk of a man standing behind the bar. Tears filled her eyes. Her hands shook when she reached for his cheek. "My God, it's good to see another brother free." She sniffed, then continued. "Akira will be so happy."

"Akira, is she still alive?" Ian grabbed May's shoulders as he demanded. "Tell me, where be my sister?"

"Akira isn't alive, my *brathair*," Gavin answered, meeting Ian's questioning gaze across May's head. "Her spirit chose to linger, condemned to protect us."

"I doubt Akira sees it that way," May snapped, spinning free of Ian's grip and turning toward Gavin. "The key word there is *chose*. She chose to walk this world and you should be damn grateful that she did. Without her, you'd still be cursed."

"Aye, milady. I suffer gratitude and remorse. Without her, it would be no freedom. It is my fault that her soul hath sought no peace. It is a twisted path I follow in search of my *brathairs* to set them free and ease my sister's burden, so she shall seek rest eternal."

"I vow my strength in this crusade, my *brathair* Gavin," Ian replied. He stood to full height, chin tilted proud, his right hand fisted over his heart.

He looked like a buff-bodied warrior to Izzy, making her heart flutter. But they weren't at war. The image of the form she filled out to join Brother Leod's strange gang floated through her thoughts. Then again, she stared from brother to brother, maybe they were.

Chapter Nine

ဆာ

The appetite Ian took to the table was that of a starved man. Izzy watched him polish off everything on his plate three times and down more mead than Colin. And that was a feat. Where Colin's words were slurred, his nose was red and his eyes were mere slits, Ian's speech went unhindered and his features did not change. Throughout the meal, the discussion of the curse and the amount of time that had passed was nonstop. His interest in the electric lights was nothing compared to the amazement he got out of the bar taps. Colin took pleasure in demonstrating how they worked over and over.

Izzy sat comfortably on the barstool with her laptop. In the tavern, it was hit or miss with a wireless signal and dial-up was slower than slow. Somehow, she got lucky. Ian's words replayed in her head and she was dying to know what he said, even though she had gotten an idea of their meaning from his actions.

My dona boireannach, you have me cruaidh 'n acras for your sheath.

She guessed at the spelling as she typed the words, and hoped the translation site figured it out. After several seconds, the translation appeared. Her jaw dropped.

He called her a naughty woman, who had him hard and hungry for her pussy.

Did he think that was romantic? Izzy bit her lip and tried to stifle the rush of laughter that rose at his odd attempt to woo her. Rereading the words gave her a new perspective. He was hot and horny for her, just as she was for him. She sat upright, staring at the translation, thinking each word through.

Being called a naughty woman wasn't a bad thing, albeit not the most romantic, either. But it had sounded rather sexy when he spoke to her in his native tongue with that sensual, smooth Scottish tone.

His speaking dirty in Celtic should upset her.

It didn't.

His blatant whisperings about being balls deep inside of her before the night was over, in a normal situation, would have been considered distasteful. She would have slapped him. But this wasn't normal. He wasn't normal. His wordage didn't offend her, instead it tripled her excitement. Izzy squirmed on the stool at that thought. Ian had her moist between her thighs without even touching her. Before she forgot, she typed in something else he had said.

Dona leannan. Instantly, the site translated the words to mean naughty lover.

Now that was something she liked. She could live with being his naughty lover. Naughty woman sounded too old and stuffy to her. Izzy turned on the stool to face the table where he sat. Watching him eat made her think that food was food to a man, no matter what the century.

When he caught her looking, he grinned, lifted the fingers she knew he had stroked her with, and wickedly licked them. Heat seeped up Izzy's neck as she hesitantly glanced around to make sure no one saw. Certain that no one had, she decided two could play that game. Glancing around, she saw Margaret, Ned, May and Ericka engrossed in conversation over another riddle from Akira's diary. Her dad and Gavin sat across from Ian, with their backs to her. Colin stood beside Willy behind the bar, discussing some sport to bet on.

Shifting just right on the barstool, she had Ian's full attention. Izzy slid her hand under her skirt, fingering her slit in a swift motion that Ian didn't miss, but everyone else did. His gaze followed her every move. The smile on her lips couldn't be helped. Knowing he stared had her hot and horny.

Seeing his pupils dilate and his tongue dart across his lips when she ran her finger across her lips, then slipped it quickly in and out of her mouth caused her nipples to harden. Damn, she hadn't expected that reaction.

Ian's nod of approval intensified her need. Without stating a word or moving from his seat, his heated gaze reinforced his claim that she would be his this night. Izzy swallowed hard as the realization hit her. She was playing with a true sexual master. Anticipation rippled through her system, switched her nerves on high, drained her mouth of moisture, yet flooded her sex with her juices. Oh God, could she handle this?

Staring directly at him, she decided, *oh yes*, she could and would.

Once his hunger for food and drink was quenched, he wanted to see his home. Angus gave Ian a t-shirt with the tavern logo on it to wear. Its triple-x size was snug, formfitting to his chest, biceps and abdomen, making Izzy's breath hitch in her throat. Dressed in a red and green kilt, ancient leather boots and a tight white t-shirt sporting an overflowing mug of ale engraved with a Celtic cross might go unnoticed on the street. But the huge sword draped at his side was an issue.

It took quite a bit of convincing from Gavin to relieve his brother of the weapon. But it didn't happen until Ian was assured that he could keep his *sgian dubh*, which was safely tucked in his boot. Ned placed the large sword in a blanket he retrieved from his car to disguise its appearance, then took it outside and placed it in the trunk.

When they walked outside, Ian stiffened and absently groped for his sword. Wide-eyed, he turned his head from side to side. Two bright eyes shone from the front of a beast, the likes of which he had never seen. Another appeared down the road from the tavern. Did they travel in packs? Without his weapon, how would he defeat these beasts? In one stealth motion, he retrieved his *sgian dubh* from his boot. Though small and slender, its sting was sharp.

"*Brathair*," Gavin spoke in a calm level manner as his hand landed on Ian's shoulder. "There is much you have to learn of this world. This is not a beast before you, but a machine called a car and it is the mode by which we travel."

Ian stared from the car to Gavin, then back to the car. He stood motionless, watching as Gavin led Ericka to the beast, opened its side and helped her in. By the heavens, Gavin was feeding his woman to the beast. Ian's breathing increased, his heart pounded and his nostrils flared. Was his *brathair* mad? Peering inside, he saw Ned in the front holding a round object. Ericka looked uneaten as well. Not even a drop of saliva appeared on her being. The touch of a hand on his arm made him jump back and away from the metal beast.

"Ian, it's okay," Izzy said as soft and as reassuring as she could. She tried to put herself in his place. An eighteenth century Scotsman awakened a few hours earlier in the twenty-first century. Things were definitely different to him. Nothing was how it was when he was cursed. This had to be hard for him to understand.

"Aye, Ian," May said as she slid into the backseat beside Ericka. "It's faster than a horse to the castle. You'll see. Get in."

Ian looked at Izzy. The man was confused. For an instant, she thought she read fear in his eyes before an unreadable shield slid in place, hiding his inner feelings, replacing them with emotionless eyes. *Just like the eyes from her dream.* A tremor shot down her spine. Was this the real Ian? A man of no feeling? No, Izzy shook the idea from her thoughts. That was not her Ian. Her Ian? What had gotten into her? Just because she freed him and they had a few fleeting moments of heat. Granted, they were the hottest seconds of her life. It didn't make him hers.

Looking at the hunk of hot Scottish laird, she knew what controlled her brainwaves and her libido. Izzy forced her gaze from Ian long enough to see Margaret slide into the backseat next to May. If Gavin got into the front seat, that left little room for Ian.

"Come, my *brathair*," Gavin called as he motioned for Ian to climb in beside the woman. "Let's be off to Castle MacKinnon and get you settled at home. I know Akira's spirit be anxious to see you."

Before she thought better of it, Izzy sputtered. "I'll take Ian in my car. It looks kind of tight in there."

"So be it," Gavin said, shut the door and turned to Ian. "I'll see you at home."

He slapped Ian in a brotherly hug, then got into the car. For several seconds, they stood watching the car drive away. The sound of people walking down the street snapped Izzy out of the haze. They didn't need to see Ian. Ian was new. They didn't know him, and at the moment, Izzy felt it was best to keep him out of harm's way.

Her dad and she were on the same frequency. It was as if they connected without words. Instantly, he stepped beside Ian.

"It might be best if you leave with Izzy, before the town realizes they have a visitor." Angus nodded at the three men ambling at a slow pace toward the tavern. "Not everyone's apt to understand the curse as we have."

Izzy hurried Ian to her car, opened the door and practically shoved him inside. The car was small and his legs were cramped. At his size, he'd be cramped in almost any car. She slammed the door and scurried to the driver's side. They pulled away from the curb just as the tavern regulars arrived at the doorstep. In her rearview, she saw her dad, Colin and Willy escort the men in like it were any other night.

Silence fell between them. Izzy noticed his white-knuckled grip of one hand on the seat edge and the other on the dashboard. Her first instinct was to laugh, but she managed to swallow it at the sight of his tension-filled face. Ian sat rigid, taking short shallow breaths. It was obvious to her that he was terrified, even if he wouldn't admit it.

Should she say something to try to soothe him? Unable to think of the right thing to say, she remained silent and drove, forcing her gaze to the road. Maybe he needed the quiet to soak in the changes to the village and the countryside. It was dark, so how much could he actually see other than what was touched by the glow of her headlights. When she reached the end of Main Street, she turned left onto the road that wound its way further up into the mountains and to the castle.

Surrounded by darkness on the outside and the low light from the dashboard on the inside, Izzy knew he couldn't see much. She cleared her throat and found the courage to speak.

"Ian, you okay?"

"Aye." He answered, but gave no further information. She wasn't sure if she should continue to strive for conversation, or leave him be. Deciding to try, she continued.

"Just thought you'd like to know, my metal beast hasn't taken any prisoners or killed anyone, ever," she said. Out of the corner of her eye, she thought she saw a partial smile and hoped it was a good sign that maybe he would relax.

When he didn't reply, she tried again. "If you want to talk, ask questions, you should know that I'm here to help. It's got to be a strain for you, waking up in a world two hundred years older and not understanding the particulars of how things work."

Silence lingered for what seemed like forever before he spoke.

"What do you feed your beast?"

Izzy smiled, at least he was talking. "A car isn't alive. It doesn't eat. But in order to make it go, you have to fill it with petrol and keep the engine tuned for better mileage."

"I do not understand this petrol and engine. There is much I do not understand." His voice sounded weary and Izzy's heart sank.

"You can't expect to learn it all in one night. There's been so much that has happened, since you were cursed." Izzy paused. She wanted to help him in any way that she could, and not just sexually. He seemed like a lost kitten in a massive field of tall grass, uncertain which way to turn to find his way back to a place of comfort and safety. "I'm sure once we get you back to the castle you'll feel more at ease. That's one place that hasn't changed much since you lived there. Your sister made sure of that."

"How so? My sister's a spirit."

Izzy had to think fast. As a child, she'd heard the tales of the haunted castle, but never truly believed them. And even though Ericka explained about Akira's ghost being confined to the castle until her last brother was found, Izzy still wasn't sure of its truth. Ghosts weren't real. But hadn't she seen her mother's spirit. Hadn't that spirit guided her and helped set Ian free. That seemed real to her. Curses weren't supposed to be real either. Looking at Ian, she knew that curses were real, or at least this one was, because a MacKinnon sat next to her in living, breathing form. In order to answer his question, Izzy relied on the stories Ericka had shared with her as they waited in the Internet Pub earlier.

"While Akira lived, she dedicated her life to maintaining what was left of the MacKinnon clan. Which wasn't much, since Hume MacGillivray made sure he cursed all of the brothers and killed Gavin's wife."

"Tavia." The single word whispered on a sad breath from Ian's side of the car. Izzy waited, but he said nothing else. She licked her lips, took a deep breath and stared straight into the darkness that was cut only by her headlights. Telling him this was harder than she expected.

"Akira lived at the castle with her husband and many of his family members. She had two daughters who married and moved into other clans. But she never left, not even after her husband died and his family members spread out throughout the countryside. She stayed to protect her secret. She hid Gavin in the castle. There was no way she would fail to keep him safe. In her heart, she knew that he was the key to bringing back her family, her brothers. In death, she chose to linger and walk the castle grounds, protecting him until the time came that he would find freedom. Throughout the decades, she scared away anyone who attempted to renovate the tower she kept him in. The rest of the castle has been updated, but not the center tower."

"Gavin's tower," Ian said. "It was his rightful place as leader of the clan. The tower to the back right of Gavin's, how has it been changed?"

"You'll see when we get there, which won't be much longer."

Izzy noted that Ian released the dashboard, but not the seat. At least that was some progress in getting him to relax.

"I believe you speak the truth of my sister's spirit. As a young lass, she was a mischief-maker and headstrong. She kept Gavin and me busy protecting her virtue. Many a young lad aimed to tip our sister, but only one earned the right. A lad named Malcolm MacDonell."

Izzy straightened. Both hands tightened on the steering wheel. Malcolm MacDonell. Were they somehow related? Was Akira her great-great-great-grandmother or something like that? *OhmyGod*, her eyes widened as her breath halted. Had she been diddling with a distant relative? She had to know. Without thought, she sped the car up. This was bad. She had the worst case of the hots for a possible long-lost relative. Though after two hundred years the true blood relationship was lost, she still didn't like the idea that he may have some connection to her. It was a situation she intended to clear up before she'd let this go any further.

Within minutes, they reached the castle. Ericka, Gavin and May stood outside waiting to greet them. A loud puppy hopped at their heels, barking. Izzy leaned across Ian to open the door. The brush of his chest to her arm sent chills down her spine. She bolted upright, ashamed of her body's reaction. Damn, she sighed, rolling her eyes heavenward and issuing a silent prayer. *Give me strength to resist temptation, please.*

Izzy got out of the car and walked to where the others stood, making sure not to touch Ian in any way, shape or form. After May introduced them to Belvedere, her English Springer Spaniel puppy, he quit barking and pranced as if he were their guide. They walked inside and she followed, bringing up the rear. Big mistake. Ian walked in front of her. No amount of effort kept her eyes off his arse. The moment the thought, *wonder if he'd like it if I nipped him on the arse*, flashed through her brain, she almost stumbled into him. Need for distance and control kept her upright and an arm's length from his back.

A large tapestry on the wall caught her attention and granted her a reprieve from staring at his beautiful backside. All seven brothers stood behind three women seated on a bench beneath a large tree. Gavin was the tallest, situated in the middle. Though he was handsome, it was Ian's presence in the picture that captivated her gaze. She knew the tapestry was over two hundred years old, but its colors, style and accuracy in their features was amazing. Even after all these years, it remained intact.

"It is the real man which stands behind you, my *dona leannan*." Ian whispered in her ear. His heated breath tickled her skin and sent arrows of renewed need to bulls-eye in her core. The hooded gaze he gifted her with chipped at the miniscule resistance she grasped for control over.

Avoiding him was going to be harder than she thought. Izzy rendered another silent prayer for strength. The moment his hand cupped her elbow and guided her to follow the others, she knew her resolve weakened. Would her soul be condemned to hell if she fell to the sin of incest? Not that she was promiscuous. She wasn't exactly angel material, either. Sexual experiments tended to remain among her circle of close friends at university. Never to her knowledge had she crossed the line of incest or had relations with married partners. That had to account for something, didn't it?

Skimming her gaze down his body, she wondered how bad hell really was in perspective to her soul. Was Ian worth the risk? If the tremendous pressure building in her sex was any clue, she sensed that he was, even if her mind refused to grasp it.

When they entered the parlor, a bright light flashed, a chill filled the air and a ghostly figure appeared. The vision was slight of build with bright red hair and brilliant green eyes. It reminded her of one of the women on the tapestry.

Belvedere jumped and barked until the transparent woman ran a hand down his back. That seemed to be enough for him and he curled up beside Aunt May's chair.

"Ian," its voice seemed to screech, excitedly. "My *brathair*, you are free."

Ian kneeled at the feet of the hovering image. "My sister, there is much that I owe thee."

"Nay, Ian." Akira's transparent hand brushed his brow as she spoke. "it was nothing you would not have done for me."

"Do you not wish to seek your rest?" Ian's brows pursed as his gaze remained fixated on his sister's ghost.

"My sweet *brathair*, as I have explained to Gavin, my rest shall come, when my last *brathair* is free. That was the vow I made at death with the guardian of souls."

Ian spun to face Gavin. "Then we must not hesitate in their recovery. We must find and free them. Akira deserves eternal rest."

"Aye, that she does. But the task isn't a simple one. Our *brathairs* were hidden with the help of many hands. Each gave Akira a riddle with which to seek them when the time came."

"Their time hath come," Ian stated with his gaze locked on Gavin's, as if challenging him to say otherwise.

Ericka interrupted. "It isn't that simple. The riddles were given to Akira without the answers. Each clan held on to that part as an added measure of protection. Unfortunately, over the years many of those clans no longer exist. The answers have been lost. It's up to us to figure out the riddles and learn the others' locations. And believe me," she said as she pushed back a loose strand of auburn hair from her face. "It isn't that easy. We got lucky with you because of Izzy. She found you first."

The power of Ian's gaze nearly knocked Izzy off her feet. There was no mistaking the look. He wanted her, and if she didn't figure out a way to gain control over her rampant sex drive, there was no way she would stop him. Incest or not, she wasn't sure if she had the strength to deny the ravenous lust he caused within her being. Just looking at him made her weak.

After Margaret and Ned left for home, they spent several hours showing and teaching Ian the changes made to the castle. From electric lights to new kitchen appliances to the wonders of indoor plumbing, it was like dealing with a child. His questions were exhausting, but between Izzy, Ericka and Aunt May, they were able to shift the burden from one to another to keep up with him. In the early morning hours before daylight, he decided it was time to see his tower. He grabbed Izzy's hand and tugged her into a standing position.

"Come, Izzy. Show me the far tower." He glanced over her head in Gavin's direction. "It is still mine, is it not?"

"Aye, Ian. You still be the right hand of the family. The tower still be yours." Gavin turned to Aunt May as he added. "Isn't it?"

May laughed as she spoke. "Of course. The deed may list me as the owner, but this is still MacKinnon Castle. I just live here." She winked as she stood and gathered Belvedere in her arms. "Now if you'll excuse us, we're off to bed."

"Goodnight, Aunt May," Ericka said as she brushed a kiss to her cheek and tousled the puppy's ears. "See you in the morning."

Gavin stood as if to follow Ian when he started for the tower, but Ericka stopped him. Her subtle nod in Izzy's direction didn't go unnoticed by Gavin or Izzy. But before she could request that they join them, Ericka shut down that plan with Akira's help.

"You two go on up. We'll be here when you get back. I want to go over something with Gavin and Akira that I read in the diary." She gathered Gavin's arm in her hands and led him back to the couch, while Akira's ghost simply smiled.

Ian had her out the door and down the hall before Izzy could utter one protest.

"Do you think that wise to send them off alone?" Gavin asked.

Ericka and Akira shot each other a look before laughing.

"My *brathair*, did you not notice the *sùgadh* between them."

"*Sùgadh*, ye sure?" The look of dismay on his face set them into a tirade of laughter.

"I can't believe you didn't see the attraction between them. You know for the curse to be truly broken, it requires true love to shatter the stone around the heart." Ericka rolled her eyes when he shook his head. "Men, it's a wonder they ever clue into the intricacies of love and relationships."

Akira nodded her agreement. Gavin laid his arm around Ericka's shoulders and tugged her close to him.

"*M'Gaol*, you need no proof of my attraction for you. As for the intricacies of love and relationships, I'm up for a lesson, if you be so willing to teach."

The subtle action of Gavin laying Ericka's hand in his lap covered by his own, didn't go unnoticed by Akira.

"Ugh," she moaned. "You definitely need help in the wooing of a woman, my *brathair*."

With that she disappeared, leaving Gavin and Ericka alone in the parlor.

"You know," Ericka teased. "I don't think we've made love in here yet."

"That be a situation we shall right this night."

Chapter Ten

ဆဝ

Dead man walking, echoed in her head as Ian led her through the corridors to his tower. The further away from the safety of the others in the parlor she got, the more her gut twisted. She wanted him. He wanted her. Not a bad thing, if it were up to her raging libido. Incest flashed like a bright red neon sign in her brain, causing her to shiver.

"My *dona leannan,* are you cold?"

Before she could answer, Ian's arm wrapped around her shoulders. The heat of his touch soothed her chills, while at the same time, it managed to slice off another layer of her thin resolve to resist the temptation of his sexual heat. Each step closer to the archway of his tower increased the rate her sex throbbed and lowered her resistance level even more. When he paused in the doorway, she knew she was going straight to hell the moment his lips brushed hers in a tender kiss. If she didn't try to stop this now, she was doomed.

"I..." She paused, gathered her strength and forced the words to exit her lips, which was hard to do with him standing face to face with her. "We can't do this."

Ian grabbed her wrist, tugged it to the front of his kilt and rubbed her balled fist against his hard-on. "My *dona leannan,* you can not leave me like this. You had me *cruaidh 'n acras* for you all night. Don't tell me you are nothing but a tease."

Never had anyone called her that before. Izzy didn't tease and not go through with the actions. This was different. She had to make him understand before he hated her. The temptation of his cock was too great. Before she thought better of it, she had to touch it, just once. Open palmed, she examined his impressive package through his kilt while attempting to explain, as best as she could, as to why they had to stop. Though at the moment, there wasn't one ounce of her that wanted too.

"Ian, did Akira's husband, Malcolm MacDonell, own Grant's Tavern?" The words came out on a hoarse whisper. It amazed her that she'd managed to ask the question, while caressing his clothed cock in her hand. Part of her brain needed to know the answer, while the raging libido part wanted nothing more than to taste the salt of his cock with her tongue.

"Isabo, it is not the time to speak of such." Ian's voice was gravelly and rough. The passion filled gaze that met hers pinned her to the wall. Any other time, Izzy would have crumpled to her knees and giving her all to please him. She refused to buckle to her needs or his...not without knowing if they were kin or not.

"Ian, I need to know this," she demanded, her voice hoarse with need. Her grip tightened and Ian straightened.

The pleading look in her eyes and the urgent sound of her voice cut through the fog in his brain created by her hand on his shaft. Her fingers were magic, caressing him to near release. If she continued, he would be spent within a matter of seconds. Maybe it was a good thing she wanted to talk first. At the tavern, she hadn't struck him as a woman of words. She seemed more of a woman of action to him, which was the type of woman he liked.

Ian searched her face as if it held the reason for her sudden need to know the answer to a question that made no sense to him. Lowering his gaze, it lingered on those full red lips, making him hunger for a taste. If he delved into them, would she forget the question and give into his needs. The quick dart of her tongue across her lips made his cock twitch in her grip. When she shifted her grasp, he knew he was lost.

Whatever she wanted to know, he would tell her and hoped it earned him a tumble between her thighs.

"Malcolm did not own the tavern. It was his younger *brathair*, Fergus. A fine man that one. He ran a grand place, good mead and fair gaming. Now what has that got to do with this?"

Izzy ran the scenario of her family tree inside her head. There was no MacKinnon blood in her heritage. Akira wasn't her great-great anything. Thus, it wasn't incest. And if she'd thought it through in the first place, she would have realized Akira had no male offspring. The tavern had been handed down from one male MacDonell to the next for generations. Relief flooded her system as an unstoppable bout of laughter ripped from her throat.

"Lass, have you gone mad," Ian clasped her head in his hands as he spoke.

"No," Izzy managed to sputter as she regained her composure. "I had to be sure we weren't related. When you said that Akira was married to a MacDonell, I thought she was my distant kin. You see, Grant's Tavern has been in my family since it was built."

"We are not kin, lass. Shall you be my *dona leannan*, now?"

Ian emphasized his meaning by pressing his pelvis against her abdomen and rubbing his cock up and down the sensitive clothed flesh. Electric shocks rifled her system and accumulated in her pussy, drowning her thong in moisture. Hot and unable to speak, Izzy simply nodded her consent.

He gathered Izzy in his arms and carried her into what was once his tower. Izzy flicked on the light switch as they entered the room. Nothing of the old remained except for the fireplace with its solid mahogany mantel. Ian froze. Modern furniture filled the room. Matching brown leather sofas sat facing each other in the center of the hardwood floor. At each end of the couches were accent tables with Tiffany lamps. The lamps contained remarkable hunting scenes etched in the stained glass.

In slow motion, Ian lowered Izzy and held her around the waist, snuggled close to him as she gained her balance. Together, they stepped forward until they stood at the edge of the huge white rug situated on the floor between the couches. He released her. She watched him walk around the couches as if uncertain about stepping on the bright white rug.

"Ian, this is beautiful," Izzy said.

"It is not as I left it," he stated as he moved about the room.

At the mantel, he ran his hand along the wood. Memories flooded his thoughts. That piece of wood he worked with his own hands to make it the center of his fireplace. It stood out among all the others in the castle. He spent weeks shaping and smoothing it to perfection. Was this all that was left of his prior existence? A piece of wood.

Ian turned on his heels and paced the room. Books lined the shelves on the wall to the left of the entrance. Scanning through the titles, many he could not read, but a couple of tattered spines stood out located on the top shelf. He couldn't believe his eyes. The two he favored from his time remained. As if they were more fragile than a newborn, he slipped them from the shelf and held them in his hands, staring at the titles written in Celtic. Aye, the passages were a sight to his eyes as he opened the favorite of the two.

An unstoppable smile upturned his lips as he read his favorite poem. When Izzy moved beside him, he closed the book and tucked both back up on the shelf out of her reach. It would not do to have a woman know his weakness for the poetic word. Nay, *strong men did not read such.* The words of his father reminded him, causing his mood to darken. Absently, Ian rubbed his jaw to stop the phantom sensation of the one and only punch his father had ever managed to land. But it hadn't been enough to knock the hate out of him that wrapped around his heart from the damage caused by Siusan.

In sudden need of space between him and Izzy, he walked to the far wall and stared out into the darkness, leaving Izzy to continue examining the bookshelf. The fight that drove a spike between him and his father, Farlon MacKinnon, replayed inside of his head. A mere lad in love with a woman he could not have. Though he was young, he wooed her and thought he'd won the fair maiden's hand.

He was mistaken.

On the very eve he planned to ask for her hand, his father announced his upcoming nuptials. Shock and disgust controlled his every move that night. The woman on the dais beside his father was the woman he loved, Siusan. Though they had never been intimate, it killed him to know that she would share her body with an old man, night after night.

Never would he forget or forgive her for such a betrayal. Her claim of not knowing Ian's intent still stabbed at his heart. Part of him decided she knew, but chose the position as the lady of the MacKinnon clan that being married to his father entitled her. The other part simply died, closing off his heart against any further chance at destruction.

Women were playthings. He'd convinced himself of that as a way to prevent another female from getting too close. Good for a tumble and not much more. He snarled at his reflection. Closing his eyes, he mentally shoved the painful memories back into the darkest crevices of his conscious.

He stood with his broad back to her as he stared out the windows. That long dark hair was loose and made her fingers itch to touch its silken strands. His taut stance with his legs slightly apart and his hands on his hips set her imagination on fire. What was he thinking that had his shoulders so tight? Wondering if he wore anything under that kilt had her moist between her thighs and she shifted, trying to alleviate the sudden discomfort of her thong.

Slowly, she lowered to her hands and knees, and crawled across the floor as stealthy as a cat seeking its prey. Inch by inch, her gaze traveled up the back of his calves to his knees, then up to the majestic shape of his rump in that kilt. Damn, she was horny and wanted him now. He was a hunger she desperately needed to sate. Licking her lips, she glided to a stop just behind his strong legs.

Before he could register what she was planning, she slid her hands up his calves to his knees, then grasped his firm, muscular thighs underneath his kilt. For an instant, his gaze seemed startled when their eyes met, then instant heat pooled within his irises right before she maneuvered under his kilt, hiding her head from view. The heat of the tip of her tongue left a trail of scorched skin as she tortured him slowly, working her way to his front while remaining on her knees.

Ian's cock twitched and hardened as she massaged it from root to stem. Just holding it in her hands made her feel powerful and purely sexual. His stilted gasp urged her on as he grasped her shoulders. Izzy continued to caress his cock as she licked the sensitive skin underneath from the base to its tip. Circling the thick head with the tip of her tongue, she coaxed a drop of pre-cum to peak from its slender orifice.

"Uhm," she moaned, licking the glistening tip. "Tasty."

"My *dona leannan*," rumbled from his lips as he lifted her to her feet. "I'll show you what's tasty." He growled against her lips as he captured her mouth.

Waging a passionate war on her mouth, he slowly backed her up against the floor to ceiling window. As he lifted her against the cool glass, she wound her arms around his neck and wrapped her legs around his waist, keeping her thighs open as wide as possible while still holding on. Izzy's short skirt slid up her thighs, exposing moist pouting, pink lips for his viewing pleasure. His pupils dilated, his nostrils flared and his tongue darted across his lips as he stared at her sex. It was obvious he liked what he saw, which made Izzy squirm, rocking her pelvis in a teasing motion.

"You like what you see," she teased in a husky voice.

"Aye, it is a fuck'n pleasurable sheath splayed open for my cock. Let's see if you are ready to be filled." He growled as he slid one thick finger along her soaking slit, moving the thong to the side before burrowing knuckle deep into her warmth.

Izzy gasped, then captured his mouth in a furious kiss as he worked her into a heated frenzy. In and out, his finger worked her pussy, coaxing her inner muscles to spasm and coat his skin with her juices. Though his finger felt good, she wanted his cock. Never had she wanted a man inside her as much as she wanted it now. Ian was the one. The one who would give her the ultimate orgasm, this she believed with all her heart.

In a slow seductive manner, she trailed the fingers of one hand down his chest to his rock-hard abdomen, then lowered to gather the front of his kilt into a bunch between them. That majestic male member of his jutted straight from a nestle of dark curls and she moaned when the head thumped her mons, sending more of her juices to flood that perfect finger of his, which was strumming her clit into a measure of painful pleasure.

Ian slid his slick finger from her heat and lifted it to his lips. He suckled it into his mouth as if it contained every ounce of nourishment he would ever need. Izzy licked her lips, unable to look anywhere else but his mouth. The sight of his finger coated with her juices being licked by his sensual tongue made her hunger for his kiss.

When he'd licked his finger clean, he smiled at her and said, "Now that, my *dona leannan*, is tasty."

Grasping her hips tight, in one swift movement he plunged into her sheath until he was seated to the hilt. Her sharp cry stung his ears as surprise registered in his soul. Ian froze, unable to move. Never had he been gifted with such. And coming from this one...it was a total surprise. The way she sucked his cock and fondled his balls, he never would've expected her to be...

"Isabo, ye should've told me," he whispered against her brow.

What was he going to do now? He'd taken her maidenhead. This was the one gift given to a husband on their wedding bed, it was why he'd never received such a present. Marriage was a feat he managed to avoid. In his day, this meant marriage. Would her father seek such from him? Never had he made such a mistake in his judgment of a woman before. Only those skilled at pleasure entered his bed.

Now he had tainted Isabo's virtue. What did this mean in this world of hers? Though every ounce of him begged to continue, to fuck the beauty in his arms, he couldn't.

Izzy tilted her chin and met his concerned gaze. Every ounce of her hummed with need. He couldn't stop now. Not with his cock inside of her and her pussy wanting more. The initial pain eased. It was time for the pleasure she'd waited so long to experience. For some reason, she'd saved herself for him and she wasn't about to miss out on the greatest orgasm of her life. Not if she could help it.

"Told you what?" Izzy swallowed hard and forced a control to her voice that she didn't feel. She was perched on a perfect cock, waiting for sex and he chose now to show concern for her virtue. "That I've had sex every way imaginable without total penetration. Ian, you wanted this as much as I did."

Slow and deliberate, she rocked her pelvis the length of his cock. Tremors shot up her spine when she pushed, filling her sex to the hilt with his cock once again. She grasped his head in her hands and rasped on a heated breathe.

"Show me what it's like to be fucked by a real man, Ian. I want an orgasm that'll blow my mind."

He did not understand this *blow my mind*, but he knew how to fuck. Unable to resist her blatant invitation, Ian captured her mouth as he took over the pace. In and out, slow then fast, he pumped his hips, working Isabo into a majestic creation of perfect pleasure molded by his skill.

Since this was her first time, part of him wanted to make it memorable and fuck her like she wanted. But a small part of him wanted to be gentle with her. She was his first virgin. Should he go slow and easy or pound into her the way every ounce of him wanted to? Would he hurt her if he did?

When Izzy fisted his hair in her hands, rasped, *Fuck me harder,* in his ear, then nipped his shoulder with her teeth as she rocked like a wild *dona leannan* on his cock, he lost control. Their motions intensified. Pound for pound, she met his thrust, gasping and nipping at the flesh of his ear, neck and shoulder. Never had any of his prior *leannans* ever treated his flesh in such a manner.

The quick nips of her teeth added pain with his pleasure. Did he like it? The moment she latched on to the base of his neck, suckling and nipping the tender flesh, his cock throbbed harder in response and he decided that he liked her passionate tasting of his skin. But he felt she deserved a similar pleasure.

Breaking free of her mouth on his neck, he captured her nipple between his teeth and tugged. Her audible moan let him know she liked this added maneuver. Ian suckled and nibbled, tugged and bit from breast to breast until Isabo's gasps were ragged and shallow. Her nails clawed into his shoulders as if she clung to him for dear life. Her legs tightened around his waist, and when the heels of her leather boots dug into his butt cheeks, he relinquished control.

Wave upon wave of spasms tugged his cock deeper into her sheath, causing his balls to tighten even more. The phenomenal strength of her orgasm cascading across his shaft guided him into the hardest release of his life. Never had his seed exploded with the force that it did wrapped in her warmth. But it didn't stop there.

Isabo surprised him once again. After several seconds of lingering, lost in the moment of sheer bliss, she released the grip she held around his waist with her legs. His hands slid up her body as she lowered to her knees and took the plump, thick head of his cock into her lush lips.

Ian nearly crumpled when she suckled the last remaining drops of his seed from his well-worked cock. Virgin or not, where was a woman like this when he was a younger man?

When she released his cock, her gaze glistened from passion as their eyes met and she whispered. "I had to have a taste."

Her wicked smile hinted of more pleasure to come, but Ian read the exhaustion in her face. Glancing out the window, he saw the signs of the coming of sunrise. Soon the sun would break the sky and it would be dawn.

Tomorrow he'd have her again. Now she needed her rest. Ian lifted her into his arms. "Come, my *dona leannan*, let me take you to bed."

With Isabo snuggled in his arms, he found what used to be his room at the top of the stairs. Nothing in here was the same either. In the center of the room, a king-sized canopy bed sat with a nightstand on each side and matching lamps. His foot seemed to sink in the plush pile of carpet that coated the floor, making him weary in his steps. The sensation beneath his feet was odd.

Cradling Isabo in one arm, he pulled down the blanket and laid her upon the downy soft mattress. What it was made of, he did not know, but he liked the texture. Her eyes closed the moment her head touched the pillow, making him smile. Her expression looked so gentle. Ian clasped first one, then the other of her boots in his hands and tugged them from her feet. After removing his boots, the t-shirt and his kilt, he crawled naked into the bed beside her and snuggled close to her warmth.

She rolled onto her side, then snuggled and shifted into the safety his large frame wrapped around her provided. Ian pulled her close and whispered against her hair, just before he fell asleep.

"Isabo, what am I to do with you now?"

Chapter Eleven

ജ

Bright sunlight warmed Izzy's face. Sleep filtered from her system as she stretched, chin tilted into the sun's heat. Last night was the best night of her life. She sighed, relishing in the memory of the phenomenal orgasm she accomplished with the help of Ian's masterful skills. He had been worth the wait. Izzy's brow bunched as she thought that through.

Had she truly waited for Ian?

Thinking back, the recurrent dreams she suffered throughout her life weren't meant to torment her. They were meant to remind her of the magic that waited as long as she saved a portion of herself for him. Had her mother's spirit implanted that idea in her head when she found Ian's statue as a child? She felt certain that was the truth behind it. An unstoppable smile crossed her lips as she issued a silent word of thanks for her mother's insight on that one. Saving her virginity for Ian had been the best accomplishment of her life.

Izzy moistened her lips, tasting a hint of Ian's flavor lingering there. She sighed. She was in need of another sample of her Scottish laird. Though they no longer touched, the dip of the bed weighted down let her know he was still lying behind her. In a slow, seductive manner, she rolled over to face her man.

Her man, just the thought had her giddy with anticipation. When had she started thinking of Ian as such? After great sex, of course, she admitted as she inched the sheet from over his face. For a split second, her heart stopped and her lungs failed to function. Her jaw dropped. Both eyes widened at the sight and the scream that tried to escape became a gurgle in her throat.

.

129

Instinct took over, forcing her limbs to scoot her backward until she fell off the bed onto the floor. Sitting up, she peeked over the edge of the bed. OhmyGod, it wasn't a dream. Seconds turned into minutes. All she could do was stare, unable to move. Was this some sort of cruel joke?

His eyes were closed as if he were only asleep. His gallant form lay on its side. One muscled arm curled under the pillow, the other splayed palm open on the bed near where she had lain. Daring to look, Izzy lifted the covers. Ian's top leg was bent at an angle, covering his penis from view. The thought that he had snuggled behind her naked renewed the ache in her sex for his cock.

Slowly, she crawled back onto the bed. Trembling fingers stroked his rock-hard cheek, then lowered to trace his lips. That mouth had given her such pleasure. Would it ever again? Izzy bit the edge of her lower lip. Did he taste the same in this state as he did as man? Her gut knotted as she leaned forward, touching her lips to his. Rough stone grated the tender skin, and yet she pressed harder. Heat sizzled from the motionless mouth, causing Izzy to curse as she shot upright.

Damn, what happened? Had she truly felt warmth? Both hands fisted the sheet, twisting it into a tangled mess. Never had this much confusion possessed her brain. Should she kiss him again or should she not? Determined not to act like a schoolgirl on her first date, Izzy gathered her resolve and delved in for another brush with fate. Again, her lips burned at the touch, but she was ready this time and absorbed it instead of running from it. A hairsbreadth of separation between them, she studied his sleeping features. He appeared at peace, whereas in the form she found him in at the tavern, he portrayed a fierce warrior. This way he was more at rest, she reasoned, trying to accept this latest twist to the MacKinnon saga.

Why had he turned to stone again? Hadn't she spoken the words that were necessary to release the curse? These were questions she desperately needed the answers to and she knew who had them.

Izzy slid from the bed, stood upright, straightened her clothes and grabbed her boots as she marched from the room and down the stairs. Barefoot and carrying her boots, it took her no time to exit the tower and locate the kitchen. She followed her nose, which was captivated by the scent of breakfast. The growl of her stomach reminded her that she skipped the evening meal. After the workout Ian had given her the night before, she was famished.

Margaret led her to the veranda, where Ericka, Gavin and Aunt May were gathered. Ericka and her aunt were seated at the table, while Gavin stood with a cup of steaming hot coffee in his hand. Its aroma teased her senses. Coffee was a definite need this morning. Gavin was the first to speak.

No good morning, no hello, just point-blank he stated. "Ian returned to stone, didn't he?"

Stunned that he knew, Izzy nodded her reply. Before she found her voice to speak, he turned to Ericka and continued. "I told you my *brathair* is not an easy man. It will take mor'n a night to win his heart, if ever."

"You weren't exactly easy, my love." Ericka said and smiled as Gavin stiffened. His expression displayed one of feigned disbelief until Ericka laid her hand on his. His gaze quickly switched to playful passion. Their teasing camaraderie had Izzy wishing for the same.

Would she and Ian have a similar instantaneous relationship? Ericka and Gavin had not known each other long. Granted, he had only been free of the curse a short time. Looking from one to the other, Izzy sensed that they were perfect for each other. Their actions were in sync. To her, they seemed as if they had been a couple forever.

When Ericka continued, Izzy returned her gaze to Ericka's face. "From the heat I sensed between you two, I'd hoped that Ian would be easier to reach, than Gavin."

Izzy's eyebrow arched. This had taken a twist for the even more odd than ever in her book. She licked her lips, then asked, "What do you mean by reach him? Why did he turn back into a statue? I thought you said that all I had to do was speak the words and he'd be free."

The air turned ice cold, sending chills scurrying along her spine. Akira's image appeared in a bright flash of light next to Izzy, making her jump. If it wasn't for Gavin's quick reaction, she'd have landed on her bottom. Once he was sure she was steady, he let her go.

"Akira, you and I both know the light flash is all for show. Cut it out. You're scaring the lass." May quipped as she stood, walked over to the sideboard table and poured a cup of coffee. "Lord knows she's been scared enough."

"May, you take the fun out o' everything." Akira stated in a playful huff as she settled on the garden wall which lined the outer edges of the veranda.

"Here, Izzy, it looks as if you could use this," May said, handing her the cup.

"It is only half a freedom," Akira said in a hushed voice, gazing out over the field of wildflowers, rocks and hills. "Ian is free by night, but not by day."

"What are you saying? That Ian's still cursed!" Izzy screamed as she spun to face Ericka. The fast movement sent coffee spilling over the edge of the forgotten cup in her hand. "I thought you knew the anti-curse, that all I had to do to free him was speak the words. I spoke the words. Now look what's happened," Izzy sputtered, trying to contain her temper, "he's locked inside a stone walled prison. Can he breathe? Does he know where he is?"

"Lass." Gavin's hand covered the cup and removed it from hers as he spoke. "Ian is safe 'til sunset."

Izzy's brain hurt. Strange thoughts spiraled through her aching head. Images she didn't want to imagine popped up and refused to dissipate.

"You mean he's going to rise up out of the stone like some sort of vampire out of a coffin when the sun goes down."

"Kind of like that," Ericka explained. "You see, the curse used on the MacKinnon men was called the curse of the gargoyle. It perpetrated the myth of the gargoyle into a magic incantation which, when used, turns a person to stone. Gargoyles were mythical creatures that were stone statues by day, but at night they were guardians and protectors of the people near them."

Something didn't sound right to Izzy. According to every myth she'd ever heard, the gargoyle creature switched back and forth at dusk and dawn. If that were so and this was the basis of the curse, then why...she managed to voice the question that burned bright inside her brain. "If what you say is true, then why did the brothers remain frozen in stone consistently? Why didn't they change with the day and night?"

"MacGillivray made it so," Akira said as she floated to hover next to Ericka, facing Izzy. "He was an evil man that one, and smart. When he cursed my *brathairs*, he did not recite the full passage. The part you spoke was the part he left out."

Ericka continued where Akira left off. "You see, from what we've figured out, Hume MacGillivray must have studied the curse before using it and realized the power of that last passage of the incantation. He wanted the brothers out of his way for good. If they held the ability to seek revenge, even if it were only at night, he had the foresight to know he was a doomed man."

"Aye, he would have been a dead man if I got my hands on him," Gavin stated. His words seethed with anger and Izzy read the hatred he held in his gaze.

Izzy's head spun. Not sure if it were from not eating or information overload, she sat in the nearest chair. Thoughts were flipping through her synapses at a rapid rate, to the point she was certain her head would burst. Digging her palms into her temples, she attempted to combat the rise of pressure and sort through the massive jumble.

"You all right, lass?"

Gavin's voice sounded concerned as he handed her a glass of water. She didn't speak, just nodded, then took a swig and set it on the table. Several seconds ticked away before the missing link in the information she'd been given surfaced. She took a deep breath and scanned from face to face as she spoke.

"How did he know this curse? Where did he get it from?" Izzy narrowed her gaze on Akira as she stated the next question before her first two were answered. "And most of all, how did you learn which curse was used on your brothers?"

Akira crossed her transparent arms over her chest in a matter-of-fact-way and returned Izzy's stare. But it was Aunt May who answered.

"I know you know of the Book of Shadows. I know Ericka told you about it. Hume MacGillivray found it hidden in the monastery that took him in when he left the MacKinnon Clan. When he learned of the black magic powers of the incantations noted within its pages, he stole it and used the passage he felt would help seek his revenge against the brothers. But it wasn't enough to just curse them to stone. He wanted to destroy the statues as well." May turned a heartwarming gaze to Akira as she said. "If it weren't for Akira's quick thinking, he would have succeeded too."

Akira took over where May left off.

"MacGillivray tried to correct his mistake o' leaving me alive. He sent a man to kill me. The man he sent did not believe in MacGillivray. You see," Akira floated closer to Izzy as she spoke. "MacGillivray led the brotherhood with fear. Any who did not follow his command, he punished by placing an evil spell upon them and their families from the book. This man hid his family, then delivered the spell he stole from the book under the guise o' killing me. This man risked his life to correct what he felt was a wrong. It was wrong for

MacGillivray to control those men that way. It was wrong what he did to my family."

Izzy watched Akira's face sadden as she asked. "Why didn't you use the spell to release your brothers? Why leave them in stone?"

"It was half a freedom. Stone by day and free at night. What kind o' life was that for my *brathairs* to lead? I spent the rest o' my life searching for the answer, the spell that would free their souls completely. Near the end o' my time, I carved the last passage in a slate and placed it at Gavin's feet. My last breath was a prayer for their freedom. It is why the heavens have allowed me to linger, to protect my *brathairs*."

Pure unadulterated respect bloomed in Izzy's heart for Akira. This woman was ahead of her time. She gave everything she had to protect her family during an era in Scotland's history where women were considered weak and fragile, simple possessions to protect. And here the role had reversed. Akira had been the protector, the one with the brains to outwit a madman. If she had lived during Akira's time, Izzy felt certain they would have been friends.

"What happened to MacGillivray? Please tell me you kicked his arse," Izzy said, then grinned at Akira.

"Nay, the heavens took care o' him. The devil slipped and broke his neck when he fell down a flight o' stairs."

"It was unfit he died that way," Gavin declared. "He deserved to be disemboweled by the hand of my ancestors."

The image of Gavin gutting a man flashed through her thoughts and Izzy swallowed hard as she stared him, up and down. Did he have it in him to kill a man that way? Did Ian? Gavin's stance, tightened jaw and evil glare hinted that he did, sending chills to her arms. True, MacGillivray had wronged the MacKinnons. But did that give Gavin the right to hunger for blood revenge? In 1740 Scotland, it did, Izzy decided as she realigned her train of thought and continued the line of questioning that she desperately needed answered.

"What about the Book of Shadows? Where is it and do you think it contains the anti-curse that would release them completely?" Izzy knew she grasped at straws with that question. Akira was smart and would have thought of it already, but she had to know in order to strike it from the growing list of possibilities in her head. There had to be an anti-curse out there, knowing where had already been searched would save her the trouble.

"The brotherhood claimed they destroyed it after his death. They did not wish it to fall in the hands o' another devil man. Until recently, I believed that as truth."

"Brother Leod wants the book." Ericka repeated some of the information she had given Izzy earlier, but it was her next words that grasped her thoughts and knotted her gut. "If he gets to it before we do, there's no telling to what extent he may use the black magic that's supposed to be concealed in its pages. Once he's destroyed the MacKinnon clan as he claims he wants to do, what next? How far will he take this? We've seen a small portion of what that book contains. There's no telling what its powers would make him capable of doing."

* * * * *

The drive home from the castle was a blur. Ericka's words resounded in her head. *How far would he take this?* Was Brother Leod really a madman bent on world domination? Oh God, she thought on a heavy sigh. This sounded like a bad movie script.

What was worse, Ericka and Gavin managed to sidestep her questions about how he was freed from the curse. Had they found the anti-curse and for some reason didn't want to share it with his brother? No, Izzy shook her head. There had to be another answer. Gavin seemed dedicated to finding and freeing his brothers, so he wouldn't keep the key to freedom from them. Or would he? That little smidgeon of doubt had her hurrying homeward. She needed her computer, the internet and a shower, but not in that order. If Gavin refused to share the antidote, then it was up to her to find it.

Izzy was glad that her dad wasn't home when she got there. All she wanted was a shower and a chance to think things through. But the shower didn't help. Every muscle, every nerve ending ached with the need to help Ian and his brothers. There had to be an answer. Something was staring her straight in the face, but she couldn't see it through the fog of jumbled thoughts that matted her brain.

After dressing, getting a quick bite to eat and downing two aspirin, she headed to the Internet Pub. She needed to open in order to maintain the appearance that life was normal. Izzy huffed as she unlocked the pub door. Life for her would never be normal again. Not with Ian around. But would he be a part of her world? Would he fit in?

And what bothered her most, would he be hers? A man as good-looking as Ian could have his pick of any woman out there. Once acclimated to the differences of today, would he still be interested in her?

If he didn't, Izzy decided as she booted up her laptop, at least she had one hell of a night to remember.

Her fingers trembled across the keypad. One night would never be enough. Already she was hungry for another taste of Ian's lovemaking expertise. He was different from any of her male friends. The group that she and Nessia hung out with at university made a pact to experience sex to whatever extent they each wanted, as long as it was kept among the six of them. The rise in sexually transmitted diseases in young people led them to their decision of creating this sexual haven of sorts. At the time, it seemed like a safe solution to sexual exploration without ending up titled a whore or scarred by some disease. Now Izzy wasn't so sure it had been the right move.

Damn, she hated feeling like this. She rolled her eyes upward and issued a silent prayer for strength and guidance. Never had she regretted anything she and her friends had ever done together. She took a deep breath, gathered her resolve and decided she wasn't about to start second-guessing her sexual escapades. Oral had been her favorite both in receiving and giving, whether male or female friends. It hadn't mattered. Sex toys had also come into to play, but never had she used a rubber cock for more than clitoral stimulation or an anal fuck. And in that department it had only been a slender vibrator that got her off. The larger ones hurt.

If Ian knew the extent of her experiences, would he still want her? Izzy bit her lip as she closed her eyes, envisioning Ian's face when she caressed his cock in her mouth. He loved it. There was no missing that fact. And she loved the taste of him. Thinking about his thick, juicy cock had her mouth watering. His was larger than any of the others she had tasted. Licking her lips, she couldn't remember the taste of their cum. But Ian's she savored and hungered for more. No, she wasn't going to regret a thing that she had learned. Instead, she planned to share these sexual tidbits with an ancient Scotsman.

Thinking of him tied to the bed being tickled with the tip of her tongue made her shiver and her nipples jutted into hard points. Izzy opened her eyes and tried to force her concentration on the computer screen. She had the day to track down as much information as her skilled fingers could acquire from the internet highway. But what would she do at sundown? The tapping of the keys stopped. The pub was opened 'til ten every night. How could she do that and still see Ian? His time was limited and she wanted to grasp every second of it that she could.

This was something she would have to think about. Before she could, an e-mail caught her eye. The snake had sent a second reply to her application. Since she hadn't taken the time to effectively read through the first one, she decided to read it before opening the second one.

My Dear Applicant,

It humbles me at the extent of the replies to my offer. Yours will be given due consideration. Each applicant shall be given challenges to prove their worth to our society. Those who pass each test shall join. Those who fail shall not.

You will be contacted with the date, place and time of our first meeting. Due to the nature of our society, all contact must be kept secret. Anyone who divulges the nature of our beliefs shall be dealt with accordingly.

Until We Meet,

Master Leod

Master Leod? Who the hell did he think he was? Izzy screwed up her face at that one, then remembered he wasn't quite right in the head. Skimming down to the next e-mail, she noted the time sent. These were less than twenty-four hours apart.

Inez,

It gives me great pleasure to honor you with the title of first chosen. Your challenge awaits. Friday night, at the stroke of midnight, be at Darkest Desires, a tavern of Gothic nature located on Berners Mews, London.

Until We Meet,

Master Leod

Izzy sat back, staring at the blinking cursor. What was she going to do? Friday was just a week away. If she didn't go, she'd lose the chance of not only catching the man who burned down her dad's cottage, but she'd also lose the chance to end the feud against the MacKinnons. There was no way she was going to lose either. Should she present this new information to the others? What if she was wrong and this wasn't the same man?

No, she decided. This was something best handled without their involvement. She wouldn't confront him with her suspicions. Instead, she would keep the appointment, but not meet the man face to face. She was certain that she could recognize him. All she had to do was show up and determine from a distance if it was the same Brother Leod who attacked Ericka, tried to kill Gavin and burned down the cottage in his efforts. If it was him, she'd alert the authorities. Izzy decided her plan of action. Several of her college friends lived in London. A club like this one was just the place they'd love to go. They didn't have to know what she was up to. When she was done with this e-mail to Brother Leod, she'd send e-mails to her friends and invite them to meet her there for a night of fun.

Before she convinced herself otherwise, Izzy replied.

Master, just typing the word made her skin crawl. Deceit was the single way into this special society, so she wrote what she thought he wanted to hear. There was no other way for her to find out what she wanted to know. She had to be accepted as one of their kind if she was going to pull this off. Izzy took a deep breath to settle her nerves, then continued.

There is much I hope to learn from you, A sly smile crossed her lips. That part truly wasn't a lie. If this went as she hoped, she'd walk away with the anti-curse. That was, if he was the Brother Leod that they were after.

'Til then.

Your Faithful Servant,

Inez

It almost made her gag to write that, but she did. She was no one's faithful servant, much less his. If Ian wanted her to dress like a maid or servant, well, that was another fantasy altogether.

The thought of wearing a tight little black and white French maid costume and servicing Ian in any way he liked had her hot and moist between the thighs. Did he like to play sex games? That was something she'd have to find out. Role-playing had been a part of her sexual experiences that she enjoyed. Would he?

Glancing around, she noted the pub was still empty. Not unusual for a weekday before noon. Izzy slid off the stool behind the counter and entered her small office. She needed a minute. Ian was in her head, making her skin itch for his touch and her pussy wet for his cock. There was paperwork that needed attention. She hoped it'd engage her brain in financial matters and swerve her thoughts from Ian and his magnificent cock for at least an hour or two. But she doubted it. In her heart, she knew there was nothing that would ever take him off her mind completely.

* * * * *

Ian woke to the sensation of Izzy's sweet lips upon his. Though he tried desperately to respond, he couldn't. His lips would not move. His hands did not function and his eyes refused to obey and open.

By the heavens, where was he?

When he fell asleep, he was in his bedchamber with a beautiful woman in his arms. What had she done to him?

He struggled to breathe, but could not. It seemed as if his body lay locked within a solid prison of darkness, yet his mind was awake. His eyes would not obey and open. He sensed nothingness filled the space around him.

Was Isabo near? In an attempt to soothe his rampant thoughts, Ian focused on her face and the kiss he knew he felt when he first woke. Isabo had kissed him, of that he was certain. But what happened to place him in this cell of pitch black was not within his grasp of understanding.

Had the curse been placed upon him again?

Ian wanted to scream, to reach Gavin for answers, but failed. Nothing followed the commands of his brain, not his mouth, not his eyes, not one muscle could he move.

Pure frustration filled his next thought as the worst Scottish curse words he knew flew through his brain. *Cuntybuggeryfucktoleybumshite!*

Ian, curb your tongue, Akira stated as she slipped inside his stone prison.

Akira, where are you? Why can I not see nor move?

You are safe, my brathair. It is the curse. You are not totally free.

Explain, Ian stated, trying to control his anger and dismay. It would not do to upset his sister's spirit, since she seemed to be his link with the outside of this prison.

You be free by night, but not by day. It is the way of the curse.

Och! This is a horrible state in which my brathair and I lie. Gavin, is he safe?

Aye, Akira hesitated, then chose not to tell Ian of Gavin's freedom. Knowing how Ian's heart was hardened toward love, she doubted he'd ever be truly free of the curse. *You shall see him at sunset. Rest. It is all you have until dark.*

Ian hated being trapped. To lie here entombed in a stone shell was trying his patience. He needed out. He yearned to touch the beautiful Isabo again. All thought stopped. Isabo...

Akira, is Isabo safe?

He waited for her answer as if it were the key to open his cell. The odd-looking virgin had gifted him with a memory he would cherish for eternity. But what of her outcome? Had she been cursed for having lain with him?

Akira! He screamed in his thoughts. She had to still be near. He had to know. Several seconds ticked by before she replied. Her voice seemed distant and tired.

Ian, I can not be slipping between the stone and the outside world. It is not good for your soul nor mine.

I have to know if you want me to rest. Is Isabo safe?'

Aye.

The one word answer was enough to soothe his soul. For reasons he could not grasp, knowing that Isabo was safe eased a portion of stress from his thoughts. Confinement was not his favorite place to be.

Ian forced his system to calm as best as he could. Visions of people and places he would never see again flashed through his thoughts. Sadness wrapped around his heart, though it did not beat. Hume MacGillivray destroyed his *brathairs* over a woman. This he knew as truth. Gavin married Tavia, the woman Hume claimed to be his. Gavin won her heart. Hume won her friendship, which wasn't enough.

Did that give Hume reason to curse the MacKinnon males? Nay, Ian decided. Women were not a reason to fight over nor curse another. A woman was a reason to fuck. Nothing more. Nothing less.

A dark-haired young lass filtered into his thoughts, though he tried desperately to prevent it. Her smiling face glowed behind his frozen shut lids. Siusan was supposed to be his and not his father's. Losing her hand to his father made him bitter and turned him away from love, he determined as he rifled through those painful memories. Why he felt this way, he could not remember. Had it been love or simply a matter of a young lad's lust? Or was it the fact that the old geezer had beaten him as he had in many other games of challenge throughout his young adult life?

What was it about losing Siusan that turned him to drink, games and whores?

Aye, he thought. She was a lovely maiden. But try as he might, he could not remember her kiss. Had their lips ever touched? Ian shuffled through his deck of memories. Nae, he wanted to taste her mouth, but the moment never arose. The closest he'd ever gotten was a chaste kiss to her hand. That did not matter. Ian determined as he huffed angrily inside his head.

What did matter was the flavor that taunted him now. Ah, the fine young Isabo. His anger fizzled as her image appeared, erasing Siusan. If he could move, she'd be beneath him with his cock buried deep within her warmth.

Bright red lips that tasted of sweet nectar, the practiced tongue of a whore, combined with long legs and full round breasts fitted perfect for his mouth had him hungering for more. True, her short spiked white hair and her clothes were odd, but her green eyes were commanding. Each pump inside of her snug, wet sheath made those eyes of hers shine dark green, commandeering his gaze and not allowing him to look elsewhere. Watching her expressions of ecstasy as he made her his up against the glass had been raw and real.

What was he to do with her now that he had taken her maiden flower? Fuck her, that's what. The words screamed through his mind.

If he could get hard, Ian knew his cock would be primed and ready for another taste of his *dona leannan*, Isabo. Och, just thinking o' her had him dying to get out of this solid rock prison. The phantom feel of her thighs hugging his waist as he plowed into her tortured his brain. Round juicy nipples tickled his tongue. Her fragrant scent of arousal teased his memory.

Nightfall was an eternity away. His body was unable to respond, but his brain was swollen with need. Isabo ruled his thoughts. Sex filled his senses and kept his synapses firing. Thoughts of his hands on her breasts, plucking her nipples with his teeth and hearing his name moaned from her lips when his thumb stroked her clit gave him the fuel he needed to forget his surroundings and wait out his new enemy...daylight.

Chapter Twelve

ℬ

Luck smiled on Izzy the moment the Fergusen twins walked in the door. She spent the day tending to a few customers on and off, but mostly searched the internet for the anti-curse to Ian's dilemma and daydreamed about sex with him. If anyone knew how to run the pub other than Izzy, it was them.

Striking a deal with them was the best thing she could have ever done. They would work as a team after their homework was done until closing time. In exchange, she would pay them a small allowance each, along with free unlimited internet access as long as all the customers were waited upon. Izzy spoke with their mum on the telephone and it was agreed that they would start that night. By six o'clock, she had them well versed in how to close the store and where to lock up the receipts and cash. She gave them her spare key and left knowing that the pub was in good hands. Thinking back, she should've done this a long time ago. Those girls knew the computers in her place almost as well as she did.

For the first time that she could remember, she actually watched the sun begin to set as she sped along the winding road out of town to MacKinnon Castle. The brilliant shades of oranges, reds and yellows were amazing, shading the landscape with remarkable hues and tints she'd never noticed before.

Was it because she was in love? Izzy's foot slipped off the gas. The car slowed as she stared at the phenomenal scenery. This was her home, and yet she'd never noticed its beauty. Why now? Had love opened her eyes?

What was wrong with her? Izzy shook herself, gripped the steering wheel tight and floored the gas pedal. It was great sex, nothing more. Ian rocked her world and she was heading his way for another sampling of Scottish laird. And as for not noticing, well, she was older, more appreciative of her surroundings and besides, this was the first time in years that she wasn't holed up with a computer screen in her face until late night.

Staring out along the horizon, she watched the last fingers of light release its hold from around the castle as dusk settled like a cloak around its stone walls. A bolt of electrical current shot down her spine to pool in her tailbone for an instant before spiraling upward from her clit, straight along her abdomen and sizzled into her nipples, turning them rock hard. Unable to take a full breath, Izzy swerved to a stop alongside of the road. Tremors rolled from her fingertips to her toes, making her shiver, and gasp for breath.

Ian was awake. Somehow she knew this with every fiber of her being.

She had to get to him. Izzy took several breaths, trying to ease her nerves. Every ounce of her wanted to see him, to feel him and to taste him. Damn, what was wrong with her?

Somehow she knew he was free from his stone prison and that he waited for her. Then why in the hell was she sitting here, Izzy silently chided herself as she forced her body to calm and eased the car back onto the road.

Within a matter of minutes, she pulled to a halt in front of the castle. It seemed like forever before Margaret answered the door and let her in. Ericka met her in the hallway.

"Gavin went in to be with Ian when he woke," Ericka said. "I'm sure you'd like to see him as well."

"Yeah, is he still in his tower?"

"Of course."

Izzy fell into step right alongside Ericka as they walked to Ian's tower. Passing the family tapestry on the wall, she couldn't help but look at the handsome rendition of Ian and the rest of the MacKinnons. It was his image that stood out and held her gaze for the few seconds as she walked. The others, she couldn't tell you what they looked like, but Ian she could give you every detail down to the slant of his eyes.

Izzy paused and cast another look across her shoulder. His eyes seemed locked in a subtle stare at the woman she knew was his step-mother. Was there something between them? Had they been lovers? Heat simmered in her gut at the thought of Ian with another woman. Albeit, that woman was long gone and was no longer a threat, Izzy disliked her. For an instant, she slid her gaze up and down his body. His stance told a story. Or was it her imagination reading an emotion that didn't exist in his eyes? Ericka's touch to her elbow snapped her attention from the portrait, causing her to shuffle that tinge of jealousy to the back of her mind. She had no right to claim him as hers. She swallowed hard. All it was between them was great sex and that was it.

"You all right?" Ericka asked, concern filled her words.

"I thought I saw something," Izzy managed to say, though her mouth had dried.

"That's highly possible. Akira loves to play pranks. The first time I looked at Gavin in that picture, she made him wink. Of course, that was before I'd accepted the curse as real and I thought I'd totally lost my mind."

Ericka's infectious laugh caused Izzy to laugh. It helped ease the unfamiliar sensation of jealousy that had tightened her chest.

"I know the feeling," Izzy said after clearing her throat. "Curses aren't the run-of-the-mill sort of thing for me, either."

When the girls entered the tower, a buck-naked Ian had Gavin pinned to the floor, speaking in heated Gaelic.

"Ian," Izzy screamed.

"Gavin," Ericka screamed.

But it was Izzy's scream that granted Gavin the edge he needed. Ian's head snapped in her direction and his grip lessened for a second. But it was enough. Gavin flipped Ian into the air, tossing him to land against the back of one of the couches. If Izzy hadn't leapt when she did, a Tiffany lamp would have crashed to the floor. In a split second, Gavin and Ian were upright and pacing in a circle, facing each other.

Testosterone thickened the air. The sight of two ancient warriors steeling for battle graced Izzy's line of sight. Ian at full height, shoulders squared, muscles flexed in naked splendor had her hot and hungry for his touch, his taste and that magnificent cock. Forgotten was the Tiffany lamp in her hands as she stared at the vision of pure male perfection. Ericka's voice ripped her from her stupor.

"Gavin, Ian what's going on?"

"My *brathair* is a liar," Ian declared angrily. His gaze locked on Gavin's as if daring him to move.

"I told you, not to call me that, *brathair*." The words seethed from between Gavin's clenched teeth.

"How is it, milady," Ian steered his words toward Ericka without taking his eyes off his brother. "That my *brathair* is free o' the curse, yet it still befalls me?"

Ericka opened her mouth as if to speak, but Gavin interjected in a stern tone.

"It is an answer we can not give you. It is one you must learn on your own."

"Or beat out o' you," Ian spat out between clenched teeth.

Before either man could move, Izzy jumped in between them. The lamp she shoved into Gavin's fist as she spun to face Ian. Not sure what she was doing standing between two strong, able-bodied men, she just knew she had to do something or there was going to be bloodshed. Though she sided with Ian on this one, she couldn't stand the idea of two brothers beating the shit out of each other. This scuffle added to her suspicion that Gavin was hiding the truth.

But why? Now was not the time to think that one through. She had to separate the brothers, so she said the first thing that sprang into her thoughts.

"Ian, don't you think you should dress, or do you like parading about naked in front of Ericka?"

"Aye, it is nothing I am ashamed of lass," Ian quipped as he stared straight into her eyes. One eyebrow cocked and the half smile that tugged his lips warned her that his mood had an instant change even before he boasted. "You did not have a complaint last night, my *dona leannan*."

The lamp pressed into her back as she sensed Gavin tense and step as if he planned to defend her honor. But she needed no man to do that for her. Ian had no right to speak of their night together as if it were common discussion. Izzy mustered every ounce of strength she could and landed a slap to his cheek that echoed around the room.

Stunned, Ian stared at her. Never had a woman hit him before. Uncertain of how he should react, he did nothing but stand and glare. If she were a man, he'd set her on her arse. But she was a woman. His gaze lowered from her face. She stood, shoulders squared, hands on her hips. The taut buds of her nipples protruded against the belly-showing shirt that she wore. A black skirt hung low and snug to her bottom. He swore that if she shifted just right, it would slip and fall to the floor, leaving her treasure exposed for all to see.

Och. He licked his lips. She may have just hit him, but that didn't stop the rising need he had for her from concentrating in his cock. If he didn't do something soon, all in the room would see the full size of his desire. Standing there naked didn't bother him, standing there naked with a hard-on in front of his brother's woman, well, that wasn't right. Ian squatted, wrapped an arm around her upper thighs, secured his grip beneath her bottom, slung her over his shoulder, turned and marched to the stairs leading to his bedchamber.

Gavin took a step as if he planned to stop his brother, but Ericka grabbed his arm. "Let's leave them be."

"But..." Ericka shushed his words with a finger to his lips.

"No buts. Let's go and let them work this out. We both know there's only one way to break that curse and we can't interfere."

She took the lamp from his hands and replaced it to its original spot on the end table. Ericka hooked her arm in his, walked him toward the exit and added on a heated whisper. "Besides, seeing you wrestling with a naked man has me hot and horny. Think you can handle that?"

Gavin didn't hesitate as he proclaimed, "Aye, milady. It is a feat I look forward to satisfying."

The scent of Izzy's arousal taunted his nose as he carried her on his shoulder up the stairs. She squirmed as if trying to get free, but he tightened his one-armed grip and smacked her arse with his other hand. Izzy squealed. Ian's cock stood rigid. This woman had him hot and hungry for her sheath and he wasn't about to slow down or stop.

Ian tossed Izzy facedown into the rumpled covers of the unmade bed. Her short skirt lifted, exposing her lush bottom. A thin piece of material decorated with beads parted her rump cheeks and pussy lips, turning him on even more. Not giving her a chance to move, Ian grasped her ankles and dragged her to the edge of the bed. He grabbed both hips and tugged her onto her knees and toward his jutting cock. One finger traced the strand of beads of her thong and pulled it tight, digging it into her pouting pussy lips and arse.

Izzy didn't fight him. Her heated gasp encouraged his roughness. He slapped her arse and she squealed and shivered, lifting her pussy into perfect position. Moisture glistened on the beads and Ian couldn't wait. He tugged the beads to one side and thrust deep into her welcoming sex.

"Ugh," he groaned, seating his cock to the hilt and squeezing the soft flesh of her hips in his hands. For a moment he did not move, grasping for an ounce of control. It surprised him how excited her reaction to his slap had made him and how close he was to spilling his seed without first allowing her pleasure.

The woman made him crazy. Ian leaned, pressing his chest to her back. On a heated breath he whispered. "You must be punished for hitting me, *dona leannan*. How do you suggest you be disciplined? Shall I fuck you until you cannot stand or shall I tease you and leave you wanting and in need?"

Tremors cascaded the length of his fully embedded cock and Ian wasn't sure if he could pull out and leave her without fucking her. Her pussy massaged him, sucking it in deep and caressing his skin. He had to call upon the *Goddess Uathach* to grant him strength to carry out whichever punishment his *dona leannan* chose.

Pure heat sizzled in her gaze as she looked over her shoulder at him and said in a ragged voice. "Fuck me, Ian."

When she bucked against his cock, he couldn't resist. Pound for pound, he met her thrust. Slick juices coated his cock. Izzy's pussy worked his shaft, sending waves of spasms up and down it with each deep insertion. Ian couldn't get enough of this woman. She liked it rough and that's what he was giving her...hot, grinding sex.

Izzy dug her palms into the mattress and pressed her entire being into every pelvic push. Being taken from behind, roughly and angrily, increased her need for Ian's thick cock. Heavy balls slapped her clit with each penetration, sending electric shock waves up her abdomen to gather in her hardened nipples. The tight grip he held on her hips, fingers digging into her skin, bruising the tender flesh, added a hint of pain to her pleasure.

She'd played rough before, but never like this. Never with a cock plowing in and out of her pussy in furious heated strokes. The orgasms she'd experienced were nothing like the one building in her sex with each grind of Ian's hips against her backside and the sting of his balls slapping her clit. Having

Ian command her body took her on a high, hovering on the edge of sheer oblivion.

If only he'd touch that one little spot she liked, she'd reach the heaven and the stars. But he didn't. She groaned in frustration. Ache and need spiraled through her sex, controlling her breathing and the very beating of her heart. Pure heat sizzled her skin when he slapped her arse and she screamed in pleasure, shoving her sex hard against his pelvis, seating his cock to the hilt.

Unable to resist, Izzy fingered her clit, coating her middle finger with her juices. Izzy twisted with Ian's cock buried in her pussy and stared directly into his molten gaze as she positioned her fingertip. The sight of his pupils dilating as his gaze shifted and he realized what she intended to do urged her on. Ian halted with his cock nestled snug in her pussy. His hands rolled her rump cheeks apart, giving her the access that she needed.

His nostrils flared and his body tensed as she watched him watch her slide her middle finger into her arse. In and out in a slow deliberate motion, she fucked her arse and watched her man. Within moments, he rocked his cock in and out of her pussy in the same slow deliberate motion, causing Izzy to moan in ecstasy.

Faster and faster she slid her finger in and out. Ian matched her rhythm with his cock inside her pussy, until neither could take any more. Izzy's entire body jerked as her orgasm hit. She slid her finger free of her arse and leaned face-first into the mattress, gripping the sheets in her fists and wrapping her pussy tight around Ian's cock.

Sweet nectar, Ian groaned the moment her finger entered her arse. Never had he seen such. Knee-deep in drink, many a men spoke of whores who liked a poke in the arse, but never had he found a woman who enjoyed such pleasures. The sight of Izzy's finger, in and out, halted his breath and stiffened his cock, if it could be much stiffer. For a split second, he was stunned and excited by the possibilities.

Anticipation filled his veins as he tightened his grip on her arse, and matched the pace of her finger with his cock in her pussy. Faster and faster, harder and harder, he could not get enough. It was all he could do to control his release with the phenomenal sensations her finger caused to his swollen shaft. He swore he felt her movements from within against the highly sensitive skin of his cock buried in her heat.

His balls clenched, then spasmed, releasing his seed deep within his *dona leannan* the moment she screamed her ecstasy and burrowed her sex against him, taking his cock to the hilt. Her inner muscles rhythmic caresses up and down his cock sent tremors to his thighs and abdominal muscles, causing him to lean his chest against her back. He kissed her shoulder, her neck, then whispered in her ear as he scooped his arm underneath her waist and led them to their sides without easing his cock from the shelter of her warmth.

"My *dona leannan*, you are a gift of sheer pleasure."

Izzy trembled in the warmth of his arms as the heat of his breath tickled her ear. But it was his words that made her smile. He thought her to be a gift. She snuggled into him and clasped one of his hands in hers, tucking it to her breasts. Spooning had never been a thing she liked, until now.

"I think it's the other way around." She said as she tilted her chin to look at him across her shoulder.

He leaned over and brushed her lips with a tender kiss, then added. "Nay, milady, it is a good *boireannach* that brings out the best in a man in bed as in life."

Izzy swallowed hard, but held her stare at his hooded gaze. Did he mean to call her a gift of pleasure and a good woman? She couldn't be sure, so she didn't question it. A sudden chill skittered across her skin the moment Ian pushed up, slid from her pussy and eased off the bed. He offered his hand and she took it, sat up and scooted to sit on the edge of the bed.

"It is my second night o' freedom and I would like to bathe. Would my *dona leannan* teach me the ways o' your world, and show me to the bath? The bathrooms at the pub and in the downstairs of the castle have changed. I'm sure my personal bath has as well. Care to teach me its use?"

His mock curtsey had her laughing as she stood, still holding his hand. She liked being his *dona leannan* and not a good woman. Being a naughty lover was more fun. Izzy led Ian to the master bathroom connected to his bedchamber. When they entered, he froze, staring at the room.

What once held a large wooden tub and a chamber pot was now modernized. Tile decorated the walls and the floor. A gorgeous claw-footed tub sat at one side of the room, while the other side had a double sink encased in a marble countertop which was situated on a mahogany cabinet. A large shower stall with dual showerheads and surrounded by two tile walls and one rounded glass wall with a door stood at the end of the tub. Next to the window on the far wall sat the toilet.

Izzy read the confusion in his face. She knew he had been taught the basics of the bathroom changes by his brother. But she decided to go over everything in the room to reiterate its usage for him. She let go of his hand and walked around the room, explaining each object and its use. Ian was fascinated by the running water in the sink and she had to tug his hand away from the lever to get him to stop flushing the toilet. She knew he liked doing that because she'd heard him repeatedly flushing the downstairs toilet earlier. It had to be the novelty of it. She shook her head. She gave him a choice between a bath and a shower. But it was the dual showerheads of pulsating hot water that won him.

After they stepped inside, Izzy shut the door and turned to find Ian standing under one of the showerheads with his eyes closed, chin tilted, relaxing in the heated rain. Beads of water trickled down his face, his corded neck, across his shoulders, that broad chest and had his abdominal muscles glistening. Not to mention the curly dark hairs nestled at the base of his cock and balls.

Izzy licked her lips. He was a magnificent sight of pure masculinity. Instinct took over as she grabbed the bar of unused lavender soap. His eyes sprang open the moment she touched his flesh. Neither spoke as she washed his skin. Each stared at the other while Izzy lathered every inch. Washboard abs, up to his shoulders, arm pits and down his arms to his finger tips, where she playfully rinsed the soap from his skin, then sucked a finger into her mouth and caressed it with her tongue before letting it drop and continued with her task. The heated dilation of his pupils and the twitch of his cock were signs that he liked it. Signs that she didn't miss.

In a slow tortuous seduction, she eased to her knees and caressed the length of each leg from thigh, to knee, to calf, then to his toes. Soap in hand, she gathered his semihard cock and lathered from tip to stern. His deep inward gasp of air between his teeth didn't escape her ears and made her smile. Pure power surged through her veins. Izzy had him by the cock and they both liked it. She treated his balls to a teasing sudsing, before urging him to turn around to rinse and let her wash his back.

She wasn't sure who was enjoying this more, her or him. Starting at his shoulders, she worked her way down every ripple of muscle. At the base of his spine, she heard him hiss when she slid the soap between his firm cheeks. A quick reaction had her wrists captured in his hands and the soap falling to the shower floor as he spun to face her.

"Nay, that isn't a pleasure I wish to seek with you, my *dona leannan*." He grasped her tight against him. The rigidity of his cock pressed into her abdomen sent heat waves of need to her sex.

For a moment, he let her go as he knelt for the soap. The smile that spread his lips nearly melted her into a puddle. "It is my turn to play."

He spun her around to face the tile wall, placed her hands palm flat above her head and nudged her legs wide apart with his knee. The stance left her open and ready for him. Ian reached up and adjusted the showerheads so the water cascaded on both of them.

Millimeters of separation between them, he hovered. Soap in hand, he reached around Izzy and lathered her abdomen, her sides, her armpits, which made her giggle and squirm, then he lifted to her arms and trailed slowly to her neck. Dampening her hair, he lathered the short spikes and removed every ounce of stiffness. While massaging her scalp, he whispered in her ear.

"Will you grow your hair for me? Long enough for me to hold on to when we are in the throes o' passion. Hum, Izzy," he nuzzled her neck as he whispered. "Will you?"

"Aye," was the only word she managed to get past the lump in her throat. Her hair hadn't been long or its natural color of jet black since she was a teenager and had found the miracles of hair dye and scissors. But for Ian, she would grow it. Hell, for Ian, she'd do anything at the moment.

His tender caresses as he washed her body had every square inch of skin electrified. The warmth of his lips nibble her ear hardened her nipples. The flick of his tongue around its sensitive rim nearly buckled her knees, but somehow she managed to maintain the position Ian wanted her in.

The slide of the soap up and down her legs had her trembling inside. When she shifted her position, he placed his feet between hers and held them spread. His hands pressed hers tight to the tile as he stated on a heated breath against her ear. "Nay, Izzy. You must keep this stance for me. It is how I need you to be."

Unable to form words, she merely whimpered her compliance. Ian portrayed the dominant male well and had her shivering in anticipation of his next move. It was obvious to her that he liked to play sex games and this had her so turned on she was dripping wet and not just from the shower.

He rinsed the soap from her hair, then caressed her shoulders. After regaining the soap, he lathered her back, then glided the soap across her hip to her front and stopped at her lower abdomen. With his other hand, he reached around to her pouting pussy lips and fingered her clit. Her sigh had his lips back at her ear as he asked.

"You like that?"

"Aye," she replied on a soft moan as his finger swirled the swollen bud in a slow circular motion. She sensed his smile against her ear and it warmed her to the core.

Ian washed her sex and nearly brought her to orgasm. It was as if he knew just how long and how hard he could touch her to bring her close, but not close enough for completion. Hanging on the edge was killing her. His tortuous teasing set every fiber of her sex on fire and she sensed she would burst if he didn't fuck her soon.

Damn, she'd never felt this hot. Ian surprised her by leaving her clit aching and slid his hands and the soap to the small of her back. Izzy tensed. Her insides twitched, wound up tight and aching for release. The soap wiggled between her butt cheeks as Ian worked it down her sexy slit. With a thud, the soap hit the shower floor. Ian's thick finger caressed her backside before slipping between her cheeks. Hungry for his touch, Izzy arched back, spreading her legs and causing her arse to separate, giving him easier access.

One hand reached around and grasped one of her breasts as he pressed his lips against her ear and whispered. His voice sounded ragged. "Is this where you want me, Isabo?"

The feel of his finger circling her hole sent shivers to pool in her pussy. Gathering any saliva possible, she managed to whimper, "Aye."

Heat slithered down her body as she sensed Ian behind her. His hand cupped her breast in a gentle caress as his thick middle finger massaged her hidden opening. Izzy shivered.

Would he or wouldn't he? The anticipation knotted her gut until she felt the pressure and knew he'd made his decision.

As if he were afraid he'd hurt her, Ian's finger eased into her arse at a delicate pace. Izzy bit back the gasp as he inserted to the knuckle. Ian's other hand left her breast to trail lightly down her side to caress her rump. In and out, he slid. Testing her ability to stretch, he added another finger while massaging her soft flesh. Izzy's moans urged him on and jutted his cock straight.

Ian wanted more, but didn't want to hurt her. The tightness around his fingers made him hesitate, but the motion of her hips against his hand and fingers hinted she was ready. Before he could change his mind, Ian eased his fingers from her rear and guided the head of his cock to the puckered pink entrance and pushed. The door opened to him, sucking the head of his cock in, then stopped.

Her body shuddered and he feared he had hurt his *dona leannan.*

"Isabo, are you all right?"

"Ian, please," her voice trembled on a low sigh as she hesitated, then started again. Her face pressed against the tile wall, he swore he saw a tear slip free, even though they stood in the rain of the shower. "I've never had a real cock inside my arse. It's only been fingers or a slender dildo. 'Til now."

She tilted her chin and gazed across her shoulder into his eyes as she added. "'Til you."

He knew not what this dildo was, but he knew it could not be the size of his cock. Her entrance was too tight. Ian pulled out with a pop and gathered Izzy in his arms, spinning her around to face him.

"Isabo, this is twice now that I hath taken a gift from you that I did not deserve." He cupped her chin in his hand and placed a kiss to her lips.

The taste of his lips, the heat of his mouth drew her in and the pain disappeared. Everything Ian had done to her had her on the edge of ecstasy and spiraling upward until the head of his cock breached her arse. Pain took over. He was too big. A finger, maybe even two, but his cock...Part of her wanted to try it, to take all of him. But the pain had frozen her in place and made her chicken out, just like it had at university. When the other girls in their group were experiencing the height of a good butt fucking, Izzy had not gone all the way in that direction either. Never had a real cock penetrated that orifice.

Indecision rippled through her system. Should she or shouldn't she? Ian had shown her what it was like to enjoy sex to its fullest. Would it be as great as she had heard if she took him into her arse as well?

As if he sensed her inner turmoil, Ian broke from their kiss, cupped Izzy's chin and forced her to meet his gaze. His other hand washed his cock while he spoke. "This is not something you have to do for me, Isabo."

With a wag of his eyebrows, he grasped her thighs and hoisted her up against the wall. On a ragged breath, he said. "It is the heat of your sheath that my sword craves."

Izzy wrapped her legs around his waist and her arms around his neck, just in time to meet his inward thrust. Ian's cock was a perfect fit.

Chapter Thirteen

ജ

Friday morning came too soon. Izzy lay on her side, facing Ian as the first rays of sunlight peeked across the sky. In the instant between man and stone, Ian placed a tender kiss to her palm, sending an arrow of desire to spear her heart. Every morning, watching him turn strengthened her need to free him and shredded another little piece of her heart as well. She lay there staring at his eyes of stone. She laid her hand upon his rock-hard cheek and soaked in the heat that she cherished, which let her know he lived within his prison. This heat was a sign to her that he was safe, imprisoned but safe.

At the fall of night, Izzy was Ian's and he was hers. With each new rise from the stone, she was there, waiting to taste his lips, touch his skin and mount his cock. No matter how many times they had sex during the nights while he was free, she knew she'd never get enough.

Lying beside him as he lay imprisoned in stone deepened her determination to find the anti-curse. She stared at his frozen face. He was her friend as well as her lover. A slender smile tugged at her lips as the memory of him sharing a secret with her resurfaced. It was something that she knew he'd never shared with another. Together, they sat cuddled on the rug by the fire as he read to her from one of the two books in his library that were his favorites. Both were filled with verse and rhymes of poetry. It amazed her that a man such as he, a warrior, enjoyed the written works of love, nature and happiness.

The heat of the sun streaming in through the window warmed her back and she knew she had work to do if she were to help him. All week, Izzy had worked diligently with Ericka, Aunt May and Gavin. She scoured the internet searching for the anti-curse on different ancient myths and magic sites while tending the pub. Ericka popped in from time to time to help in the search, while May and Gavin attempted to decipher the rest of the riddles in Akira's diary. Of course, Akira hovered near and tried to aide in breaking the riddle's codes.

When Ian was awake and they weren't having sex, he helped decipher the clues in the riddles. Warmth grew in her gut, which made her smile broaden as she stared at his frozen form. He was so close to finding a brother. Picturing him poring over the riddle he had chosen made her brush his solid brow. The answer sat perched on the brink of breaking through in Ian's mind, but remained elusive. Izzy knew it frustrated him to be so close and yet so far from the answer.

Izzy snuggled close to Ian and savored the heat that seeped through the stone as if it were a phantom caress of his hand. An image filtered into her thoughts, causing her to rethink a few things. Last night, when Ian was tense and she rubbed his shoulders while they were in the library working with the others, Izzy caught the subtle glance that passed between Ericka and Aunt May. She sensed they were up to something. But if she asked, she knew they would skirt the issue, just as they did many times before when she'd caught them looking at her and Ian.

As if he sensed her inner turmoil, a kiss-shaped energy of heat formed for an instant on her forehead where she rested against his hardened lips. Pure joy filtered through her system at the connection that strengthened with each passing moment between them. With Ian, Izzy was happy. She dressed to please him. Short skirts, belly shirts and sexy little thongs were her normal, but he liked it best when she wore her colors. A full ladies kilt, complete with sash and white blouse had him hard the instant she walked into his bedchamber last night. She'd meant it as a sex game, a version of role-playing where she dressed the traditional Scottish lass part and he played the part he knew well...the handsome Scottish laird. After the fantastic sex they'd had last night, she planned to wear that kilt again.

Tremors skittered down her spine and pooled within her sex at the memories of their lovemaking that night. If he was in man form right now, she'd show him just how much he kept her turned on, even when he was a statue. If he wasn't a statue, she'd never have this dilemma. Izzy looked into his stone cold eyes and caressed his cheek.

Searching the internet had reaped no rewards when it came to answers to the curse. No matter what she tried, she knew what had to be done. One thing remained embedded at the base of her brain. Her scheduled meeting with the devil himself threatened her newfound happiness. It was a meeting she didn't intend to miss.

What was she to do about Ian? It was Friday. She had to be in London by midnight. There was no way possible she was going to tell him or Gavin or even Ericka about this. They would try to stop her. Or worse, they would go with her and she couldn't risk their getting hurt again by this man. She needed an excuse for not being around when he woke. Izzy flopped on her back and stared at the ceiling. Nothing came to her except the simple excuse of going to pick up a new computer for the pub. It was lame, but it would have to do unless she thought of something else later.

Izzy kissed his lips and savored the instant heat that sizzled from the simple touch. Slow and uncertain, she rose from the bed they had shared. Tightness clenched her chest as she stared at her fallen warrior. She wanted to save him from this curse. This meeting had to take place. She had to find out if this was the correct Brother Leod or not and if he knew the anti-curse. In her opinion, she had to go without them. She feared that if Ian or the others went, the results would be disastrous. If he spotted them and he was the right Brother Leod, he would disappear and their chances of learning a way to save Ian and the other brothers from the curse would diminish.

Heavy-hearted, she leaned and brushed a kiss to his brow. If she was going to be on time, she had to leave for the long trek into London by noon. That left little time to make the necessary arrangements.

One last glance at her sleeping giant and she turned on her heels and walked out the door. If she succeeded, he'd be freed. If she failed...she didn't want to think of that. Chin lifted, shoulders taut, determination set in. She would not fail her man.

And that's just what he was, she smiled as she accepted the fact. Ian was her man and she'd be damned if she'd let something like a two hundred year old curse stand in their way.

Ian sensed her move. Every fiber of his system itched to touch her, but couldn't while locked within this solid wall of rock. Something bothered his *dona leannan*. This he knew as well as he knew the scent of her flesh, the feel of her skin and the taste of her lips. Hope filled his heart that she had felt the kiss he wished to her 'n prayed it soothed whatever tormented her thoughts.

Och. He hated this prison. It was a strain upon his soul. This loss o' freedom and the hours not spent searching for his *brathairs*. Worse, he growled within his head, he could not be with his *boireannach*, Isabo.

Ian's thoughts tumbled to a halt. His *boireannach*... Was Isabo his woman? The question echoed in his brain, causing Ian to give himself a mental shake.

Nay, he did not want a woman o' his own. He warred with his inner self. A *boireannach* was good for a fuck and nothing more.

Isabo is different, a small voice whispered from within the confines of his shattered heart. She was not like Siusan. Isabo gave o' herself to him freely.

If he could smile, Ian knew he would not be strong enough to stop his lips from spreading. Just thinking of the ways his *dona leannan* had shared her pleasures with him had him aching and hungry for more o' her sweet treasures.

A woman in her colors, proud and hearty, had always touched his soul. But to see his Isabo dressed in true Scottish plaid had surprised him. Never had he reacted to the sight as he did to her. His shaft stood rigid and eager to learn if she chose to dress proper underneath her kilt.

As he had hoped, his Isabo did not fail to please him. Bare flesh greeted his hand beneath her kilt and he could not stop himself. Taking her with her colors tossed about her waist had touched his soul in a way he had not imagined...until now. Locked alone with his thoughts, the image of Isabo beneath him on his bed filled his head.

Perfect breasts peeked out from the tangled mess of her shirt and sash. Her legs were wrapped tight around his waist. His shaft nestled within the hot, moist sheath of her sex. Not once in their time together had she denied him entrance. Never had he enjoyed the pleasures o' the flesh as he had with Isabo.

Beautiful visions of Isabo flashed through his head in a nonstop multitude of sexual positions. The woman had a way o' keeping him satisfied. Her mouth was a haven o' sensual pleasure, which drained him dry when given the chance. Her sheath fit as if made for his cock. Ah, he mentally sighed. If ever there was a *boireannach* made for him, it would have to be Isabo.

Cuntybuggeryfucktoleybumshite! What was wrong with him? How had the woman slipped beneath his skin?

Because it is time to let go o' the past, that irritating little voice whispered inside of his head. But to let go was to admit he was wrong, that his father was right. Siusan never loved him in the way that he loved her. It was a one-sided affair built by the horny dreams o' a young lad.

Ian tried to think o' anything other than Isabo, but could not. Tired o' fighting his thoughts, Ian relaxed in the knowledge that no matter what happened, Isabo would be there to ease his need when he arose from the stone.

And after the day o' no rest, he sensed his need for her would be hard and heavy.

* * * * *

The bell above the door alerted Izzy to someone entering the pub. Damn, she should have locked it when she came in to route her trip online.

"You in here, Izzy." Colin's familiar voice echoed through the empty Internet Pub and she heard his footsteps heading in the direction of her office.

Her back tightened as she shuffled through the excuses in her head that she'd practiced while in the shower earlier. The internet connection at home was hit and miss this morning, so she stopped at the pub to plot her course. She contacted the twins and gave them the weekend off. All she had left to do was leave a note in the window about the pub being closed for the weekend. Colin's appearance put a kink in her plan.

Izzy took a deep breath as Colin entered her office. Lying was not her strong suit, but in this case, she had no choice. She knew that if Colin found out what she was up to, he'd try to stop her. Ian's life depended on her meeting in London and she refused to fail.

"Morning, Colin," Izzy managed to fake a chipper greeting with a smile and hoped he didn't read through it. She and Colin were closer than most brothers and sisters. They knew each other better than anyone. It killed her to have to lie to him.

. Remember, Ian's life depends on this, she silently reprimanded herself. Besides, she wasn't going to be alone. Two of her friends were meeting her there. Of course, they thought they were going to party. If everything went as planned and she spotted this Brother Leod, then she'd explain her motives to her friends. Well, not every detail, she decided. They wouldn't understand the curse thing. If it was him, she'd tell them he was the man who burned down her father's cottage and that she needed to alert the authorities. That they would understand.

"How's our man o' stone this morning?"

"Sleeping when I left." Izzy replied as she minimized the window on her computer screen, turned and gathered the instructions she printed before Colin could see them, then folded and tucked them in the leather pouch which hung low on her hips.

"Anything good you got there?"

The cock of one of Colin's thick bushy red eyebrows hinted that he was curious at her actions, so she had to think fast.

"No, just some specs on a new computer that's waiting for me in London," she said. Izzy licked her dry lips and tried desperately to portray her normal cool self, even though her insides were tied in knots. "I'm going down to pick it up. I'll be back sometime tomorrow."

"They can't deliver it?"

"They could, but it would take a couple more weeks for it to get here."

Izzy lifted her shoulders and forced her eyes to meet his. Colin's arms crossed his chest as he leaned his hip against her desk. The level-eyed stare he gave her told her that he was definitely suspicious.

"And you can't wait." He stated. In a desperate attempt to divert his attention, she grasped for a change in conversation.

"You know how much I love new techno stuff. Besides, a faster computer might help in the search for the brothers."

Izzy stepped past him, headed for the office door and hoped he would follow. When he did, she let out the breath she hadn't realized she held.

"Did you hear what those two idiots, Tim McFae and Lonnie Grooms, tried to pull on the society?"

"No," she replied, trying to act as if she cared what the village clods had been up too. She hoped to keep the conversation short. The need to get on the road burned in her gut. Somehow she had to get Colin out of the pub, lock up and leave without making him any more suspicious than she sensed he already was.

"Last night, they dragged a statue into your father's place and claimed in front o' everyone there that it was a MacKinnon."

"What," Izzy snapped as she spun on her heels to face him. Fear gripped her soul.

Few in town knew of the MacKinnon's story as being true. If these two paraded a statue into Grant's Tavern on a packed night, and claimed it as a MacKinnon brother frozen in rock, the repercussions would be serious as far as the society was concerned. The elders of this village were superstitious enough without having the idea of a curse lingering within their midst If the elders got involved, it would only add more problems than help the society. And in her opinion, one of the worst things that could happen to hinder the society's protection of the brothers was if a few of the crazies decided that the whole village was cursed too. She could imagine their reactions, especially old lady O'Reilly, parading through town, waving a cross, carrying a bible and chanting some made up verse to ward off evil while dressed in a nightgown and bunny slippers.

"Don't you worry," he stated in a calming tone as he laid a brotherly hand on her shoulder. "Your father took care o' it. By the time he was through with them, they looked like bigger fools than normal. And not one person in the place other than society members understood what was going on. Angus made sure o' it."

"And the statue," she managed to whisper.

"It weren't a brother." Colin's head shook. "It was that statue o' ole Thatcher McGee from over in Ludlow Cemetery. They stole it and thought they could pass it off for the bounty. But Angus and Ned turned the whole situation around on them, and made them look like drunken fools playing pranks. You should've seen them. Angrier than a pair o' bulls after the same mate."

Colin's hearty chuckle made her smile, even though she didn't feel it. He always was able to bring a smile to her face, even in the worst of times. But right now, she glanced at the clock on the wall, she needed him gone. She had a mission and the exploits of two dumbarses weren't her concern. Saving Ian was first and foremost on her list of things to accomplish.

"I'm sure they were," she replied as she gathered the keys to the pub off the counter and tossed them to Colin. "Mind locking up for me. I've got to get going if I plan to be back before nightfall tomorrow."

"You're serious. You're going to London to pick up a computer?"

"Yeah," she stated as she grabbed the front door to open it.

"What about your man o' stone? Won't he miss you, seeing as you have not been apart since he woke?"

Izzy stopped in her tracks. She hadn't thought this through very well. What would Ian think when he woke and she wasn't there? Swallowing hard, she didn't have time for this. She quipped as she shot him a teasing glare across her shoulder, "Jealous, Colin?"

"No, just curious. You haven't been anywhere other than his castle since that first night."

Izzy stepped toward him and caressed his cheek playfully and hoped to throw him off. "Ah, you are jealous. Tell you what," she added as she turned back to the door. "I'll call you when I get back and we'll spend the day together on Sunday. How's that?"

"Fine," he muttered as she left, but he wasn't buying it. Izzy was up to something. He felt it in his gut. They'd been friends for far too long for him to miss the fact that she was hiding something.

He followed her out the door, pretended to lock up and waved to her as she drove away. The moment she was out of sight, he slipped back in to the pub. A muffled sound in her office had him on guard. Slow and deliberate, he eased over to the door and peeked around the edge of the doorframe.

Somehow, McFae and Grooms had entered her office through a window and were printing something from her computer. Colin sprang inside.

"Now what do we have here? You two are in for a beating. You couldn't leave things be, now could you?"

He circled the desk, backing them into a corner.

"You don't scare me, Colin," Tim spat as he stiffened and squared off to face him.

Colin smiled as he readied for a fight, lifting his meaty fists and staring his opponent down. He said, "Wouldn't be much o' a fight if I did, now would it?"

Tim did the exact move Colin expected. He swung at Colin's jaw, but missed as Colin ducked and landed a direct hit to Tim's unprotected gut. Tim doubled over, gasping for air, but didn't quit. As he sank to his knees, his shoulder plowed into Colin's legs at the same moment Lonnie jumped across his falling comrade, swinging a limp-wrested fist at Colin's face.

The blow missed, blocked by Colin's arm, but the momentum sent him stumbling backward. With the wall at his back, Colin regained his balance, just in time to prevent Lonnie from hitting him with a stapler wrapped in his fist. A barroom brawl veteran, Colin grasped Lonnie's fist and twisted it, causing the stapler to hit Lonnie in the foot. The idiot screamed like a little girl at the sound of bones crunching in his wrist and hopped on one foot as if not able to distinguish which hurt him more, the broken wrist or the bruised toe.

With Lonnie out of the way, Colin turned his attention to Tim. The arse had managed to stand and pocket a sheet of paper from the printer before Colin could reach him. Colin grabbed his shoulder and spun him around, but didn't expect the solid crystal, ball-shaped paperweight to be in Tim's hand. Cupped tight, Tim landed a full force blow to Colin's cheek. At the same time, Tim's knee did the unthinkable in man upon man warfare. It connected with Colin's balls, sending them into hiding deep within his pelvis, or at least that's how it felt as the room spun and he crumpled.

"You fights like a girl," Colin growled between clenched teeth as he fought to stand. Stars shot behind his eyes as he tried to focus on the arse who was now across the room helping his accomplice to the door.

"Call it what you like," Tim replied with a twisted grin on his face. "I won."

Before Colin could move, they were out the door. Colin fell into Izzy's chair at her desk. The image upon the screen gripped his attention. They had printed the directions to a pub in London and if his gut were right, they were going after Izzy. But why? Were they that mad over Angus humiliating them over their own stupidity?

Hot streaks shot down the insides of his thighs as he repositioned in the chair. Colin swallowed hard. Now he understood why girls were told to go for the balls if they were ever in danger. It hurt worse than when he was kicked in the gut by an angry sheep he tried to shear. His cheek was swollen, but its pain was minimal compared to this.

Even though he knew it would piss Izzy off, Colin opened her files. He had to know what she was up to and he doubted it had anything to do with a computer needing to be picked up in London. Something must have weighed heavy on her mind for her to leave her computer open for anyone to access. It wasn't like Izzy to be that careless.

Three clicks and he was in her e-mail file. Colin froze, staring at the screen. All pain exited his body as he reached for the phone. He should have watched her more closely. Should have paid more attention to that first encounter she had with this pervert. Hopefully now, it wasn't too late.

"We've got a problem," he stated as soon as the other end of the line was picked up. "Izzy's headed to London with Tim and Lonnie chasing after her. But that's not the worst of it..." He paused. "She's going after MacGillivray."

Chapter Fourteen

ຽບ

Ian woke to the scent of stale ale and mead. He sat up expecting to find Isabo at his side. Instead, he saw Gavin. An unfamiliar sensation gripped his gut and tightened his chest. For the first time in days, she was not there when he woke. Where was Isabo? What had Gavin done with her? One glance around in the dimly lit room and he knew they were no longer in his bedchamber. He and his *brathair* were confined in a small box with a lit lantern swaying above their heads.

"Isabo, where is she?" he snapped as he attempted to stand. The floor beneath him shifted, keeping him fixated on his knees. Wherever he was, it seemed to him as if the small room was on the move. When his eyes managed to focus, the look that greeted him on his *brathair*'s face told him that something was wrong.

"The lass is in trouble."

Ian swallowed hard against the knot in his throat. His *dona leannan* needed him when he was unable to help her. *Och.* He thrashed a hand thorough his hair and tried to steady his nerves. Isabo was in trouble and he was in a moving box with his *brathair*. It was not the way he wanted to wake.

"Is she hurt," he managed to ask as a dozen scenarios of her demise played in his head.

"I pray that she is not."

"Explain, my *brathair*. What has happened whilst I was imprisoned?"

"Isabo has gone after a MacGillivray."

"What," Ian yelled as he sprang to his feet, bumped his head on the roof, then cursed as he dropped back onto his knees. "*Cuntybuggeryfucktoltybumshite*! Where the hell hath you brought me?"

"Ian, you must settle yourself." Gavin spoke as he pulled Ian's clothes from a bag beside him and tossed them to him. "Isabo is a strong woman. We must have faith that she shall be well until we find her. Dress. We are on our way to London. She has a meeting with a descendant of MacGillivray's at midnight."

As Ian fought to dress against the motion of the room, he continued with his questions. "What fashion of transport is this that you hath chosen?"

"In stone, you were heavy. It took four o' us to lift you in here. Angus is driving what is called a truck. He uses it to transport ale barrels for the tavern."

"That explains the smell," Ian quipped as he laid the final knot in his dress. "Any chance he left a taste?"

"Nay, Ian. You need your wits about you."

"All I need is my sword and you to point me in the direction o' the MacGillivray. If he's laid a hand upon my *boireannach*, it is the price o' his hand that he shall pay." Ian said as he whipped his double-edged claymore from its sheath and brandished it in air, enforcing his meaning.

"Your *boireannach*," Gavin stated with one eyebrow cocked as he met his *brathair's* angry glare. "Hath the mighty Ian falling for a mere woman? This is the first I've heard you call her anything but your *dona leannan*."

Ian sat back on his haunches. Was he ready to admit that Isabo meant more to him than just a night o' pleasure? Maybe, he decided, but not to his *brathair*. This was none o' his business.

"Isabo is a woman in need o' the protection o' my MacKinnon sword. That is all."

"Your sword?" Gavin prodded his *brathair*. "You'd think she'd be having enough o' your sword by now."

Honed reflexes had Ian's sword leveled within millimeters of Gavin's throat. "It is my steel o' which she needs. Nothing more, my *brathair*. It would be wise if you wish to keep your tongue for you to tame it."

Gavin eased back against the wall of the truck, crossed his arms over his chest and leveled his gaze on Ian's. But it was the slender smile that upturned his *brathair's* lips that kept Ian ill at ease. It wasn't like his *brathair* to back down, nor to smile about it. Ian sat back, but remained on guard as his *brathair* spoke.

"Ian, your sword as well as mine shall be needed in this fight. The MacGillivray o' which we speak is not like his ancestor. He hath control over a power a likes o' which I hath never seen before our last battle."

"You thought you killed him. Seems you missed."

"A mistake that shall soon be corrected." Gavin rested his arms on his bent knees as he spoke. "He hath a control over fire. It is a magic force o' some sort and he will use it against you. If he gets to Isabo before we do, he will hurt her with it. It is not a fate I wish upon anyone."

Images of Isabo at the hands of his adversary burned inside his brain. The tale that Ericka, Gavin and Akira shared with him o' their battle with MacGillivray replayed in his head and fueled his hatred. He was nae there to help them, but he was here now to save his Isabo.

His Isabo? It startled him to think of her as such. Did he consider her to be his? Ian shook his head, trying to gather his thoughts. Now was not the time to wage a war with his feelings. But no matter how he tried, he couldn't think of Isabo as anything other than his woman. And knowing that a MacGillivray was in a position to harm her fueled the heat in his gut.

"How long before we reach London?" Ian managed to state as he struggled to control his growing anger.

"Many hours, my *brathair*. Settle back, we have much to plan if we are to win this battle. But we have an advantage."

"What advantage have we?"

"Men fly in this world. After Colin helped lift you in here, he went to the nearest airport. Colin is on a flying machine called a plane, and shall reach London before us. Isabo thinks two of her friends are meeting her there. Colin found a thing called an e-mail that stated that they couldn't make it. She does not know. This information came in after she left."

"Men fly?" The thought confounded Ian, but he shook it off. Now was not the time to think of such. Isabo needed him.

"Aye, my *brathair*. It is a strange new world to which we hath awoken." Gavin sighed with a shake of his head, then continued. "But one thing has not changed."

Ian stared at the solemn look upon Gavin's face and completed his *brathair's* thought before he could. "MacGillivray is still our enemy."

Gavin nodded as he settled back against the panel truck. Frustration solidified in Ian's brain. This new world gave him a headache. Many things existed that he didn't know how to use or explain, but he did know how to fight. That could not have changed much, he decided. He was a great warrior, winner o' many a battles before he fell to the curse. Heat sizzled through his gut as the desire to spear his enemy with his sword grew to a massive internal flame. Every muscle bunched, every fiber in his being ached to fight, but he was at the disadvantage...for now.

Many hours, Ian growled between clenched teeth. Isabo needed him and he was stuck in this truck with his *brathair*, laying strategies o' war. Ian took a deep breath, sat beside his *brathair* and issued a silent prayer.

My dona leannan, Isabo, be safe.

* * * * *

Izzy arrived in the parking lot of the Gothic bar, Darkest Desires, located on Berners Mews in the heart of London's party district with time to spare. It had not taken her as long as she estimated it would take to get there. She had a little more than an hour to wait. Exhaustion riddled her body, yet anticipation and fear fueled her brain and kept her awake. Locked in her car and parked in a dark corner of the lot, she watched the patrons enter and exit as she looked for her friends. Gothic attire was not a problem. She'd checked out the website for the bar before she came and knew that most everything in her wardrobe qualified for their dress code.

Heavy-eyed, she let her lids close for a moment. Visions of Ian filled her mind. Hours earlier, when night fell, she sensed him wake. It took every ounce of strength she had to fight the urge to turn around and go back to him. But she couldn't. She had a mission.

Find the bastard who might possible know how to end this curse and set her man free.

Her man, she admitted on a heavy sigh as she lowered the seat back to rest for a few minutes. Ian was her man and she knew it. Those devastating blue eyes turned her on with a simple flash of heat and a hint of passion. That smile lured her with his devilish charms and that body. Oh, how his body dominated her entire being.

Izzy's mouth watered, making her hungry for his kiss. Her thighs tightened against the sudden need swelling in her pussy for Ian's cock. Damn, he had her heart, body and soul. Images of Ian filled her subconscious lulling her to relax, letting time slip away. The slam of a car door near her made her bolt upright. Startled, she gasped for air. She must have drifted off. *Breathe in, breathe out*, she replayed the mantra Nessia bore into her head whenever she was stressed at university. *Breathe in, breathe out*. Nerves soothed as best as she could, Izzy unlocked the door and stepped out of the car.

Ten minutes to midnight, she glanced at her watch, gathered her resolve and forced her legs to function. This Leod

MacGillivray was just a man, she reasoned. A man who was in the way of her love life. Three cars over, she stopped. What if she were wrong? What if this wasn't the same man who attacked Ericka and Gavin, the man who captured Akira and burned down her father's cottage?

Then it would just be a night of dancing and visiting with her friends, she decided. She scanned the parking lot and the line near the door, but did not see them. Had they arrived and gone in while she slept? It was possible.

Spine straight, jaw firm, Izzy continued. She sensed she wasn't wrong about this Brother Leod. Her gut instinct told her she was right. Determination fueled her steps as she strode toward the short line at the door. All she had to do was get a look at him, determine if it was him and then call the authorities. That was the plan, she reminded herself. *Don't get near him and stay close to your friends.*

Window rattling heavy metal music blared the closer she got. A huge hulk of a guy stood guard at the door, checking IDs and hitting on everything in a skirt. Izzy tugged at the edge of her black leather miniskirt, making sure it was straight since she'd dressed in the car. The reflection in the mirrored windows let her know that she looked and fit the part. She wore a short black belly shirt with a white cat skull outlined across her breasts and red and black strips on her sleeves. Hot red knee-high platform boots, a handful of gel in her hair standing it on end, ruby red lips and jet-black lined eyes had turned her back into the Gothic chick she knew so well.

Would Ian like this outfit? An unstoppable smile tugged at the corner of her lips. He would if he knew she wore the beaded thong he liked for luck. The faint memory of his fingers twisted in the beads, pulling it snug against her clit had her moist. Izzy shot her gaze to the ground and tried to shuffle her thoughts off Ian. *Breathe in, breathe out.*

In an attempt to regain her focus, she tucked all thoughts of Ian to a far corner of her brain and stepped into the back of the queue to get in. She was there for a matter of minutes before someone cupped her elbow in a firm grip. She froze, but refused to show any emotion as she tilted her chin to look across her shoulder at the person attached to the hand.

"Something you want?" Izzy stated in her best standoffish tone laced with a hint of tough Scottish chick. She kept her face deadpan of emotion, while trying to get a look at the person beneath the hooded cloak.

"You know that there is." The voice struck a familiar chord, but she couldn't place it. Not until he let the hood slip back from half of his face, while still keeping the other half shielded from view.

It took a great effort for her not to gasp. The handsome face of the man that Gavin knocked down in her pub stared back at her. It was him. She forced what she hoped came across as a smile to her lips and commanded her posture to relax. It wouldn't do to have him sense fear. In no way did she want him to think of her as a potential recruit for his demonic magical army. She was here to meet friends and that was what she intended to say to him if he asked.

In as charming a tone as she could muster, she stated. "Have we met?"

"We have." She watched the visible corner of his lips upturn in a wicked sideways smile as he added, "Online."

Izzy swallowed hard and did her best to act as if she didn't know what he was talking about. "I don't believe that we've met online or otherwise."

"It matters not what you call yourself, Izzy..." he paused licked his lips then stated. "Or Inez. But you shall call me Master Leod."

"Master Leod." Izzy was proud of herself for not gagging when she stated the name he used in his e-mails. Though she would have rather licked a toad than call him *master*. "I think you have me confused with someone else. If you don't mind, I'm waiting for my friends."

She glanced around for her friends, but didn't see them.

178

"I like the way you think on your feet. I know you came to meet me. I sense it in your thoughts." Izzy tried to remove her elbow from his grip, but it tightened as he stated. "Now, come let's go in and get comfortable."

Not wanting to lose her chance to find out what he knew about the curse, she decided to play along. It wasn't her original plan of identifying him and leaving, but if it helped her learn a way to save Ian from the curse, she'd do her best to pump Brother Leod for information. Once inside, she hoped to spot her friends and use them as a diversion to get away from him. If she didn't, then it was a crowded place. She'd kick and scream and cause a scene if she had to in order to get away. Wasn't that one of the methods they'd taught in self-defense? Izzy took a deep breath.

"Okay, Master Leod, or whatever you call yourself. Let's go in, shall we? I'm a bit chilly out here." She did her best to sound nonchalant.

"Aye, smart and beautiful. I knew you were the perfect candidate for my needs," he said. With a nod of his head toward the bouncer, he led her out of the line and straight through the door to the inside.

Loud music from a live band on stage reverberated in her ears. Thick smoke from a hundred lit cigarettes penetrated her lungs and made her cough. Red and white strobe lights flashed, blinding her for a second before she regained her focus. He was leading her through the crowd to a flight of stairs opposite the body-packed mosh pit. She didn't get a chance to look for her friends as he hustled her across the room. At the top, he opened a solid glass door, motioned her inside, then followed. Once the door closed, she realized they were in a soundproof room encased by three walls of mirrored one-way glass. A fully stocked bar, complete with a huge redheaded bartender, filled the back wall.

Deep cushioned couches sat positioned overlooking the activities below. When she tried to sit, he seemed to maneuver her to his right side before they both got comfortable. Odd, he didn't remove his cloak. Izzy shifted, trying to get a peek beneath his dark shroud, but couldn't.

He took her hand in his and warmth filled her palm. Determined not to pull back, Izzy didn't move. Ericka had told her of the heat she sensed whenever he was near. It was an evil sensation and Izzy now knew Ericka was right. The slow burn that filtered up her arm wasn't intense, but made her skin crawl. It seemed to her as if it was his rendition of some form of a test. Did he want to know if she scared easily? Was that what this was about?

Izzy licked her dry lips, then leveled her gaze on his one visible eye. It appeared to be a pleasant golden wheat color, but she knew not to stare at it for too long. Ericka warned her of his power and that somehow he controlled the thoughts of others through prolonged eye contact. So she turned her gaze to the crowd below in a casual manner in an attempt not to raise his suspicions.

"Nice place," she stated. "You own it?"

"No, an acquaintance of mine does."

"Is he a friend of yours?"

Izzy relaxed back into the cushions and did her best to ignore the growing heat from his continued touch.

"Yes, he is a friend and a believer in the ancient ways. Are you?"

When he released her hand, Izzy was relieved for the break, but it was momentary. He cupped her chin and led her gaze in his direction. His voice dropped to a lower octave as he said. "I know you registered on the website under the assumed name of Inez. You can drop the act, Izzy."

This wasn't good. Thinking only of the reason she was sitting on that couch, she decided her next course of action. Play along, find out what she could and get the hell out of there. Izzy forced a smile and stared directly at him as she answered in as convincing a tone as she could muster. "I am ashamed of my actions. I'd love to learn. Many things have always interested me, but magical forces have captured my soul."

In an attempt to remove his hand from her chin, Izzy grabbed his hand in both of hers, tugged it from her face and held it there as if it were a cherished possession and continued with her charade.

"Your website hinted to possibilities of learning to tap into the hidden magic you believe is within every being. Can you teach me to tap into my magical self?"

It was all she could do to portray an innocent in search of guidance, especially with this guy, knowing what she did about him, and not barf.

"Oh, I intend to *tap* into your magical self, Izzy," he said.

His innuendo wasn't missed, neither was the bulge in his pants as he shifted closer. Heat seemed to sizzle in the air around him and Izzy found it hard to catch a full breath. The closer he got. The hotter her temperature rose and not in a good way. Pure evil intent flashed inside her head. Pictures of flesh upon flesh, his upon hers, having sex, burned behind her eyes and she wanted to scream, but didn't.

Was he testing her again? Was he actually planting those thoughts in her head or was she imagining them? Izzy couldn't be sure, but didn't want to blow her cover. She wanted the cure for Ian's curse, and no matter what amount of pain or pornographic torture she had to endure, she was determined not to fail. It took a great effort to release his hand in a friendly manner and not drop it as if it had the plague. Izzy wiggled out of his reach and stood, giving him the best sexy-eyed gaze she could muster, though her brain burned.

"It's been a long ride. Could you show me to the ladies room? I'd like to freshen up before we..." She intentionally paused and plastered a seductive smile to her lips. The words that escaped her mouth in a faked sultry tone tightened the knot in her gut, "*Tap* into my magical muse."

"Of course," he said as he stood and motioned toward a doorway to the left of the bar.

Every ounce of her wanted to run, but she managed to maintain a casual walk and even added a sway to her hips. Inside the door, she flipped on the light switch and turned the lock. An instant feeling of safety flooded her system at the sound of the click. It wouldn't last and she knew it. She had to go back out there and ply him for information.

She turned on the water, leaned forward and splashed her face. It didn't help. The sensation of scorched skin on her chin didn't fade. Her reflection looked normal, but the skin of her face and hand where he had touched felt burned. No scars, no singed skin appeared, just the phantom sensation of heat lingered.

Izzy dried her face with a paper towel. After wasting a few more minutes pacing the bathroom, she gathered her resolve to return to her task. With her hand on the lock, she issued a silent prayer.

Please keep Ian safe, no matter what happens to me.

* * * * *

A flight delay at the beginning and air traffic at Heathrow airport kept Colin's flight circling for forty-five minutes. By the time he landed, he had less than an hour to make it to Izzy's meeting. But he would still be there before the others, if their calculations were right. The cab pulled into the parking lot of the pub, Darkest Desires, just in time for him to see Izzy being escorted inside.

He tried to follow, but was halted by a large tub o' lard who sent him to the back of the queue. This wasn't good. The line was moving slow. If the bouncer did his job and stopped chatting up every lass in the queue, he'd be inside within a matter of a few minutes. From the looks of it, that wasn't happening.

On a heavy sigh, Colin pulled the cell phone from his pocket and dialed.

"Hey, I'm here."

"Where's Izzy?" Angus asked.

"She's inside. I don't want to make a scene. I'm waiting to get through the queue. How far out are you?"

"We got lucky. Traffic was light and this ole truck made good time. We should be with you in less than thirty minutes."

"You did better'n I did." Colin said on a tired huff as he ran a hand through his hair.

"At least you're there. Can you get to her soon?"

Out of the corner of his eye, Colin caught sight of two familiar people sneaking along the wall in the shadows. What he needed was a diversion and those two would do nicely.

"The gods be a smiling upon us tonight, Angus. See you when you get here."

Colin disconnected and tucked the cell phone back in his pocket. Before either of them saw him, he stepped out of line and into the dark. Quietly and carefully, he worked his way around parked cars, being sure he kept them in sight. It seemed to him that they were hiding in the shadows near the door, waiting for the moment when the bouncer was busy and they could sneak inside.

Positioned several feet behind them, Colin picked up a rock and lobbed it at the bouncer. It connected, hitting him between his broad shoulders. The over-sized oaf spun around, forgetting about the woman in front of him.

"I'm of a mind to beat the shite out o' you for touching my woman," Colin yelled from directly behind Lonnie and Tim's hiding spot. Before either could react, he jumped forward, shoving them into the light while he remained hidden.

The bouncer responded without question. Tim ducked. Lonnie screeched as the first blow hit his already broken wrist, which the idiot held covering his face. If Colin wasn't in a rush, he would have stayed to watch the festivities. It looked funnier than a comedy show. Two sniveling jackasses battling a well-muscled fighter. He paused at the door and caught one last glimpse of the one-sided war. Tim was riding the bouncer's back. The bouncer ignored him as if he were nothing but an annoying fly, while he continued to beat the snot out of Lonnie.

Should he help? Nah, Colin decided as he slipped past the disturbance and entered the pub. Those two deserved the beating they got. His balls were still sore from Tim's well-placed girly defense and his cheek had a perfect, round shaped bruise.

Inside, the place was packed. People dressed just like Izzy filled the joint. Damn, he thrashed a hand through his hair. Finding her was going to be harder than he thought.

Slowly she opened the bathroom door, stepped out and smiled her brightest fake smile. Her prey was standing at the bar, back to her and his cloak off. Here was her chance to see what she sensed he was hiding. Within two steps of his back, he turned, keeping her to his right and handed her a drink.

"I hope you like a fine stout," he stated as he lifted his mug.

"A stout will do," Izzy replied, then returned his smile, turned and walked to the mirrored wall.

"Can they see us?" she asked, even though she knew that they probably couldn't.

"No, this room is private. No one can see or hear what happens inside."

She sensed him move. Again, he stood to her left, keeping her to his right. Izzy lifted the mug and pretended to sip. She wasn't a fool. She wasn't taking any chances that he drugged the drink while she was in the bathroom.

The phone on the bar rang and the bartender answered it. Within a second, Leod was called to the phone.

"If you'll excuse me, business."

"Of course."

From her position at the wall, she had full view of the entire pub. The mosh pit was full of bodies. Izzy scanned the crowd, looking for her friends and kept busy while he was on the phone. His voice was low and mumbled, making it hard for her to hear without being obvious that she was listening.

Straining to hear without looking like she cared, she picked up bits and pieces of his words. Fight. Parking lot. From that she figured something was going on outside that needed his attention. Izzy hoped he had to go and take care of it. His absence would give her the opportunity to think through her next step. And if the bartender went with him, her chance to search the room for clues would arise. Izzy hoped they both would have to attend the apparent fight in the parking lot and leave her alone.

A shape working its way through a section of the crowd near the door caught her attention. Colin. What was he doing here? How did he know where to find her? Izzy shuffled through the events of her morning. Their conversation was simple. She thought she convinced him she was going to London to pick up a computer. Had he seen through her lie?

Then it hit her. She never logged off. For the first time in her history with computers, she made a fatal error. She left her files open for all to see. Was that how he found her? Had he rummaged through her computer system and read her personal stuff?

Leod's heated words of "handle it" reached her loud and clear. A sliver of ice-cold chills shot down her spine at the sound of the phone being returned to the receiver. He was done with his conversation and it was clear to her he wasn't going anywhere. Disappointment filtered through her mood for an instant before she reeled it in and switched gears.

With Colin on site, she had to work fast. His presence would spoil everything.

Izzy spun around to face him. The mug slipped from her hand, spilling stout everywhere when it hit the floor. Her jaw dropped and her gaze froze on his features. Half of his face was handsome. The other half was marred. One golden wheat-colored eye stared, open wide, while the other peered through a swollen slit that was once his eyelid. His left cheek was layered in melted rows of pink and charred flesh. The hair on that side of his head was patchy and burned away in spots. His ear was singed and rolled inward, no longer a perfect match for its counterpart.

"I see you are disgusted by the work of my enemy," Leod stated as he closed the gap between them. "What he has done to me is unforgivable and must not go unpunished."

Izzy opened her mouth to defend Ian's brother, but forced it closed. Leod didn't die in the fire as Gavin had hoped, but was disfigured. After a hard swallow, Izzy managed to dislodge the knot in her throat and found her tongue.

"What enemy is that, Master Leod?"

"Why, Izzy," he stated as he brushed his fingers along her jaw and circled the spot where she stood. "We both know the name of my enemy. I smelled the MacKinnon upon your flesh the moment the breeze whisked across your skin to my nose in the parking lot. I must say, it disappointed me."

"I know no one named MacKinnon." Izzy tried to sound sincere, though the lie burned her tongue to speak it.

Lightning fast, Leod backhanded her across the cheek, causing her to step back to maintain her balance as he screamed. "Don't lie to me. I am your master. You will kneel at my feet and beg forgiveness."

Blood trickled from the cut his ring dug into her cheek. Izzy met his glare, nostrils flared, no one hit her. No one.

"You are not my master." The words seethed from between her clenched teeth. "I kneel for no one, least of all you."

This wasn't part of her plan to get the anti-curse, dump the weirdo and get back to Ian before the next fall of night. Well, she lifted her shoulders and steadied her stance, even the best laid plans hit a glitch and had to be redirected.

To her surprise, his injured eye pried open. The golden wheat color of both eyes seemed to swirl, pulling her into their erotic and dangerous dance. *Don't stare at his eyes,* whispered in Ericka's voice somewhere inside of her head. This wasn't happening. She would not fail Ian.

Visions of Leod, naked, standing over her filled her brain. Pain riddled her system as she fought for control. His hands gripped her arms, sending bolts of fire to pool in her pussy. The raw savage burn in her pelvis weakened her knees, but she refused to buckle. She would not kneel to this man no matter what amount of pain he sent reeling through her body. To kneel was to admit defeat.

Izzy fought the implanted pornographic pictures of what Leod wanted to do to her body. Sweat beaded her brow and upper lip. When his lips touched her mouth, she grappled for control of her brain waves. This man had an evil power. *Failure is not an option,* whispered through her head. His lips and tongue plundered her mouth and it was all she could do not to wretch. But if she did, would he let her go? Somehow, she doubted he would. If her mouth would follow her commands and not his, she'd have bitten off his tongue when he invaded against her will.

Both hands shook as she forced them to work. Her upper arms tingled, bruised by his grip. Fumbling fingers released his belt, then tugged at his zipper. His humping motion against her hand didn't turn her on. Neither did the images of him fucking her in the ass he placed in her head at that moment. If anyone was going to ever have that pleasure, it would be Ian, not this psycho.

Slowly and deliberately, she worked open his pants and rolled them down his slim hips along with his underwear. His audible moan when she caressed his hard-on almost made her laugh and vomit at the same time. While trying to concentrate against the onslaught of pornography he issued into her thoughts, she guided both palms down his shaft to the base. In as tender a motion as she could muster, she cupped his balls in her hands and massaged.

His lips broke free of her mouth. His head tipped back as he groaned and rocked his cock, back and forth, thumping it against her forearms. With eye contact broken, Izzy inhaled deep. Eyes closed, she repeated Nessia's silent mantra. *Breathe in, breathe out.* Courage reestablished and nerves soothed as best as possible, she knew what had to be done in order for her to escape. In this instance, she had no qualms doing it.

Strength gathered, she gripped his balls hard, squeezed and twisted. His grip on her arms lessened, his jaw dropped as he gasped. Dark black nails of one hand dug into the tender sac and scraped up the sensitive skin of his cock, drawing blood red lines. While the one hand continued to knot his ball sac, the other clawed the thick head in a decapitating pinch. If Izzy's nails were sharp, they would have removed the mushroom cap from its stem. Instead, she merely crippled the sick bastard.

Izzy released his wounded member as he sank to his knees and sat back on his heels, cradling his dick in his hands. She looked down at him and spat.

"Who's kneeling to whom now?"

At the sight of the large, redheaded bartender clearing the bar in one leap, Izzy turned on her heels and ran. She jerked the door open and made it to the landing before a massive arm clasped around her waist and dragged her back inside, kicking, clawing and screaming.

Chapter Fifteen

ဢ

Ian and Gavin pushed through the door, leaving Angus and Ned to deal with the slightly bruised bouncer and the very bloody Lonnie and Tim. Across the crowd, Ian caught sight of Colin running up a staircase and shouldering his way inside the room at the top. He nudged Gavin and pointed. Together they forged their way through the strangely dressed beings. None of the group seemed to care for their presence, but no one tried to stop them.

Ian couldn't tell who stared more, he at them or them at him.

The odd music was deafening and by the time they reached the other side, Ian's head pounded. But he wasn't sure if it was from the music or the extreme aggravation of his pent-up anger.

The brothers bounded up the stairs. Swords drawn, they stood battle ready, one on either side of the doorway. It reminded Ian of times past, when he and Gavin fought side by side to protect the lands of their forefathers, their family and their pride. Gavin gave a nod of his head and Ian smashed the glass door with one solid swipe of his sword.

When the glass cleared, Gavin shot Ian a sideways grin as he stated. "So much for the element o' surprise."

"It is over rated," Ian replied as he lunged through to the other side with Gavin at his back.

The brothers landed inside the door, battle ready. The scene stood frozen for a moment by their unexpected entrance. Colin was pinned on the floor by a large redheaded man who was in mid-punch, but had halted. Isabo had a broken bottle in her hand and was holding her own against a disfigured man. All action stopped as each stared at the brothers.

"I see I was right about you, Izzy. The stench of a MacKinnon is upon your flesh." Leod stated as a twisted smile upturned his lips.

"I'd much rather wear his scent than yours," she stated, eyes leveled on Leod and bottle neck gripped firm, waiting for his next move.

The sight of a thin line of blood on Isabo's cheek sent Ian over the edge. His vision blurred, then tunnel focused on one man as he charged toward his adversary. Three steps and the large redhead lunged in his direction. But Gavin intercepted, barreling into the meaty man at the waist and taking him down.

Leod was quick. In a smooth pirouette, he managed to grab Izzy's wrist, send bolts of molten heat ravaging through her system and force the bottle from her hand. Not to be defeated, Izzy grappled for control over the raging inferno in her body as she fisted his hair with her other hand, jerking his head backward.

At the same moment Ian lunged with his sword aimed for Leod's heart, Leod managed an incredible feat of strength, switching places with Isabo, leaving a clump of his hair in her hand. Skilled reflexes kept Ian's sword from delving deep within her chest, halting a hairsbreadth from her skin. Somehow his enemy managed to turn the table in his favor. The broken bottle was now in his possession and was pressed taut against the thumping life vein in Isabo's neck.

"Drop your weapons, both of you," Leod hissed between clenched teeth.

Gavin stood poised to plunge his sword through the bartender, but halted. Colin staggered to his feet, battered, bleeding from his lip and bruised from his round with the bartender. Ian glared at Leod, but didn't lower his sword.

Nostrils flared, heart pounding, he wanted nothing more than a fair fight with this devil spawn of MacGillivray.

"You have to hide behind a woman. You haven't the balls to fight like a man." Ian proclaimed heatedly as he watched his opponent for even the slightest of moves. One slip and Isabo's neck would be sliced. That was a sight he wished not to see.

"Whatever works," Leod replied. He dug the sharp bottle edge into Izzy's skin, drawing a drop of crimson to the surface as he added. "Your swords, drop them now."

Gavin lowered his sword and the big man rolled out of reach. Ian fisted his hilt and held his sword, unwavering and ready to plunge if Leod even shifted an ounce of flesh from behind Isabo. His brave Isabo's lower lip quivered as the only sign of her fear. Her gaze never faltered. He read her desire to win and knew something brewed within their depths. All he needed was a sign from her as to what would be the next move.

"It seems your brother is the smarter of the two of you," Leod said as he stared directly at Ian and Ian returned the glare. "You've got about three seconds before I slit her from ear to ear."

"You would eliminate your shield. And your soul would taste the steel o' my blade, before the lady hit the floor." Ian stated as an evil smirk lifted the corner of his lips. He knew he was playing a dangerous game, but he had no choice. If he lowered his sword, the devil would win and his gut told him either way, Isabo would suffer. But as long as he held his sword, she had a chance.

"Ian, it's okay." Izzy's whispered words reached his brain through the fog of anger and his gaze returned to hers. "This isn't over."

He caught the subtle slant of her eyes downward and glimpsed the metal object she slipped in a slow, non-detectable movement from a slit in the side of the leather pouch hung low on her hips. Only her fingers moved, sliding the slender switchblade from its secret compartment to cup it in her palm.

She had some form of a weapon. That was his woman. Pride filled his chest, but he refused to show it. Instead, he growled angrily as he lowered his sword and stepped aside.

"Roy, take their swords," Leod commanded to his right-hand man, who had acted as bartender. Once the swords were collected, Leod bunched the back of Izzy's shirt in one hand while holding the bottle pressed to her throat and guided them toward the broken door.

Bruised hands and knuckles caused Roy to have difficulty holding on to the heavy ancient claymores. He bobbled them trying to carry them both and dropped one to the floor at Leod and Izzy's feet.

"Idiot," Leod hissed as he stepped to her side and kicked the sword back toward Roy without releasing her shirt or the bottle at her neck.

Izzy took the golden opportunity and pressed the hair-trigger release on the switchblade, opening the knife. She palmed its handle, holding the blade end backward and swung her fisted present into Leod's side at the same time she tried to jerk free of his grip.

The bottle dug into her skin, releasing a trickle of blood from the slender cut it made before Leod dropped it. Glass shattered. Ian, Gavin and Colin sprang into action. Colin barreled into the back of Roy's knees, causing him to toss the swords into the air. Both brothers caught their swords as if they had called them to their hands. Gavin turned to face Roy.

Tucked in a crouch, Izzy was amazed and horrified at the sight. Leod pried the switchblade from his side. An angry, bright red hue filled his eyes as heat gathered in the air around him and singed her skin since she was closest to him. In his hand, the switchblade took on a new life. The steel turned a glowing orange-red, hinting of sheer heat and burned off any blood that remained.

In the instant Ian turned to face Leod, the knife was airborne, directed as if radar guided at Ian's heart. Izzy saw it before Ian. Instinct made her react. Protect Ian at all cost. She lunged from her crouched position between the two men. The force of her jump spun her in air, capturing the switchblade in her chest. She landed with a thud at Ian's feet.

Ian sank to the floor, dropped his sword and gathered Izzy in his arms. Blood oozed from the area around the knife and trickled from the slender slit in her throat. His Isabo was hurt saving his undeserving skin.

"She got what she deserved for sleeping with the enemy." Leod screeched in a high pitched, almost inhuman tone. Ian glared up at the distorted face of the devil.

Flames appeared out of nowhere, as if beckoned from the fires of hell. The couches burst into flames. Being near one of the flaming couches, Gavin grabbed Colin and jumped out of the reach of the hungry red flares. On fire, Roy rolled, trying to put out the sparks on his clothing. Leod's evil laugh echoed around the room as he spun on his heels and darted toward the door.

The need for revenge overtook his soul. Ian sprang from his position and in one fluid motion retrieved the *sgian dubh* from his boot. Practiced deadly accuracy guided his throw and buried the steel hilt deep between Leod's shoulder blades. To his amazement, the bastard remained on his feet, unsteady, but upright.

Ian tackled him, gripped the *sgian dubh* and twisted. Broken glass jabbed his legs, side and one arm as they slid through the remains of the door. Heat seared his hand as he held on to the hilt. Determination set in and he fought the searing pain in his palm. No man attacked his *boireannach* and lived.

Wiggling the blade free, he aimed to finish the devil off. He shifted to his knees and flipped Leod onto his back. The macabre face was twisted. One eye closed while the other remained open. Its odd golden wheat color swirled in a demonic pattern, setting Ian back on his heels. What sort of sorcery was this? Never had he seen or dealt with such, but there was always a first time, he decided.

"It is my honor to send you off to hell," Ian spat, grabbed Leod's hair and extended his neck, preparing to slice Leod in the manner he'd threatened Isabo.

A crash inside the room diverted his attention. One of the glass walls shattered when a chair flew through it and over the railing into the mosh pit below. Screams filled the air. The horrid music stopped. Flames followed Roy through his newly acquired escape route.

Fire! Isabo!

Ian dropped Leod's head with a bang, leapt to his feet and back into the room in a single bound. Gavin was trying to gather Isabo in his arms and help steady a badly battered Colin at the same time.

"Take Colin," Ian commanded. "Isabo is mine."

Gavin handed a non-responsive Isabo to Ian. The sight of her blood on his brother's arm hurt his heart. But there was no time for him to examine her wounds. The fire spread quickly. He knew they had to leave or the room would collapse around them. Holding her tightly to his chest, Ian followed the path of his brother.

At the spot where he left Leod, there was a puddle of blood and nothing more. Thick smoke clouded their vision and made it difficult to breathe. Luck was on their side and held the stairs long enough for them to descend before they collapsed behind his last footstep. Bodies banged into one another in an anxious battle for freedom from the flames.

Angus and Ned had every exit open and were guiding bodies out as they searched for their friends. Gavin and Colin made it to the door first. Ian with Isabo cradled in his arms followed shortly.

"Anyone left?" Angus questioned though his gaze lay on his daughter.

"Nay," Ian coughed as he struggled to speak. "We be the last."

Sirens blared in the distance. Help was on the way.

"We need to get out o' here," Ned stated. "No need to answer the law this night. This way." He scurried toward the far end of the parking lot.

"Is she..." Angus didn't finish his question as they followed Ned's lead.

"Isabo is a strong woman, Angus," Gavin answered as he helped Colin along. "But we need to seek help for her, and soon."

Tears welled in the big older man's eyes. At the truck, he gave his keys to Ned and wiggled Izzy's out of the leather pouch around her waist.

"We can not leave either vehicle here. It would be evidence against us." He turned to Gavin. "You ride in the truck with Colin. I'll take Isabo and Ian with me. We'll head to Much Hadham, which lies north o' London. I've got a cousin who owns a tavern there. His family is part o' the society. He'll help us."

Once settled in the tight fit of Izzy's car, Ian nuzzled her brow and silently prayed.

Please let Isabo live. Take me if you have need o' a soul and let her live.

* * * * *

Daylight would be upon him soon and he desperately wanted to hear her voice, to know that she survived before the curse imprisoned him. Hours had ticked away as he paced, waiting for the doctor and the nurse to come out of the room in the small country hospital. Isabo had returned from the surgical suite moments before and all he wanted was a chance to see and speak to her.

When they arrived at Angus' cousin Adam's tavern, it was obvious Isabo's wounds were more than they could handle. Adam made a call to a friend who owed him a favor. Doc Spencer, head of the local community hospital tucked in the quiet village of Much Hadham, was more than happy to oblige. Though small in size, the hospital was efficient and well maintained.

Isabo was lucky. The slit to her throat required stitches, but no vital vessels were cut. It was the knife wound in her chest that was the worry. The blade nicked her lung, thus causing it to fill with blood in the lower lobe. A tube was inserted in her chest to drain the fluid build up and released the pressure in her chest. All of this, Ian didn't understand. A woman dressed in white had explained everything to Angus, who in turn did his best to make Ian understand what had been done to save Isabo's life. The moment the doctor and nurse came out of the room, Ian didn't wait. He dodged past them into the room. He didn't have much time before he would have to locate a hiding place for his return to stone. But he had to know that she lived.

"Isabo," his voice shook, afraid that she would not answer.

He lifted the edge of the sheet and studied the wound. Large white patches covered her skin and a tube led from her chest to a bottle hung underneath the bed. A crimson liquid drizzled through the tube to the bottle and he swallowed hard, knowing he watched Isabo's life fluid drip from her body. How could this be good? But he didn't touch it. If Angus felt it was right, so be it.

Another strange thing ran from the back of one of her hands to a bag of clear liquid above her head. Glancing around, he noted there was much he did not know about her world. Ian moved to the other side of the bed and gathered her hand in his.

"Isabo, if you can hear me, please know that I am here for you." His voice cracked as he leaned near her ear and continued. "Take from me my strength, and my will to live for you needs it more than me."

He pressed a kiss to her brow. "My *dona leannan*, my Isabo, it is my heart that I give to thee."

His fingers shook as he brushed the white bandage on her neck. *Och*, how he hated the fact that the devil had gotten away. Leod did not deserve to live with what he had done to Isabo. Dark circles lay under her eyes. Her breaths came short and labored. This was not how he wished his Isabo to be...injured and unresponsive in bed.

He laid a gentle kiss upon her brow, her eyes and her uncut cheek. Her other cheek was bruised. Its cut required no stitches to heal.

"My *brathair*," Gavin interrupted. Ian hovered over Isabo. Her hand in his. He forced his eyes to turn to his brother in the doorway. "The sun rises. We must get you to the truck before its rays touch your soul."

"Aye," Ian managed to respond past the solid lump in his throat. It was all he could hope that Isabo would be safe until his return at dusk. One last gentle kiss to her knuckles and he turned to leave, shoulders slumped, head hung low. His woman lay dying and he was a condemned man, unable to help her.

Lying in the bed, she sensed his presence, but didn't have the desire to speak or return to the surface of her soul. Everything hurt. Her chest ached with each labored breath. Her throat burned and the skin tightened on her neck with each attempted shallow swallow. In her gut, she knew she failed. Ian was still cursed. The devil had taken the answer to the cure with him. Failure flashed behind her closed lids, refusing to let her surface. She failed Ian and in no way did she want to face that fact.

Then he spoke to her. Warm lips touched her brow. His hand held hers.

His words echoed in her distant thoughts. He gave her his strength, which renewed her energy. He gave her his will to live, which lit the pathway back to him. And he gave her his heart, which filled her soul with happiness and sent her racing back from the deep dark abyss she had taken refuge in against the onslaught of pain the devil had inflicted.

It took a great effort to force her mouth to move and her voice to work, but she did it. His words had touched her heart. They had reached her as she rested in a dark and cold spot somewhere deep within her soul. Isabo knew she had to return to Ian. He needed her. And she refused to let him down.

"Ian."

She had to tell him. She wanted him to know. She loved him.

The whisper was so low he wasn't sure he heard it. He froze on the spot and turned back to Isabo, afraid to look for fear that he had imagined her voice.

"Ian." Her mouth moved slightly with his name upon her lips. Ian's heart pounded.

"Isabo," he stated as he took her hand in one of his and brushed her brow with the other. "Isabo, can you hear me?"

"Aye, my love."

He watched her tongue wet her lips in a slow, awkward motion. The flutter of her eyelids stilled his breath. His Isabo was awake.

"How do ye feel?"

"Like I've been attacked by the devil." The tired smile on her lips made him smile.

"You have."

"Did we win?"

For an instant, Ian debated telling her the truth. But he decided it was best to be honest, for if he lied, she'd have his hide. Ian paused. When did he care about lying to a woman? Looking down into the most beautiful set of green eyes he had ever seen, he decided, now was when he cared. He had no reason to lie to Isabo. She was his friend, his lover and most o' all, she was his woman and he wanted to keep her.

"Nay, Isabo. He won this battle."

"Damn."

Isabo coughed and Ian slid his arm under her shoulders and lifted her a little, hoping to ease her pain.

"It is all right, Isabo. We shall win the next." Ian said, trying to calm her. He smiled down at her and it warmed his heart to see her attempt to smile back. "You need your rest. There will be plenty o' time to plan our next attack."

He lowered her back, fluffed the pillow beneath her and brushed a kiss to her forehead. Out of the corner of his eye, he caught the sun making its slow ascent into the sky through the open window curtain.

"I must be going. I'll be back, *M'Gaol*."

Isabo's grip tightened on his hand and she tugged him back down to her level.

"Ian, did you mean what you said, it's your heart that you give to me?"

The look of love in her eyes melted the cold ache in his heart and he had to admit the truth. "Aye, my *dona leannan*. It is my heart that you hold in your hands. Please don't drop it."

"Ian, I love you."

"As I you, Isabo."

Though he knew he was out of time, Ian leaned and kissed Isabo's lips, plundering her sweet taste with his tongue and showing her the heat of his passion and love in one solitary kiss. The first rays of morning light filtered into her room. Pain riddled Ian's chest and an invisible fist clenched his heart, but he couldn't pull away from Isabo. He needed her as she needed him.

Instead of breaking free from her lips, he deepened the kiss. Hunger for her filled his soul. Never could he get enough

199

of the woman named Isabo. She was his woman and he was her man.

The all too familiar sizzle of change filled the air and skittered across his skin. From the ends of his hair to the tips of his toes, he tingled and shooting arrows of heat bounced around his system. Immense pain gripped his heart, but he held his place, tasting and loving his Isabo. Lips locked together, hearts pounding as one, Ian failed to change.

Gavin stood in the doorway, in awe that his *brathair* had admitted to loving Isabo. Seeing Ian kissing Isabo in the light of the morning sun warmed his soul. A broad smile on his face, he stepped back into the hallway and closed the door. His *brathair* was free.

He returned to the waiting room at the end of the hall and sat in a chair beside Angus and Ned. Colin slept, sprawled out on the only couch in the room. His arm in a sling, battered and bruised, but alive to fight another day.

"Fine warrior, that Colin," Gavin stated.

"When he ain't on pain killers," Ned quipped as he flipped through the stations on the TV.

"The doctor said Isabo will heal. She just needs to stay a few days until they've stabilized her chest," he said. Angus glanced around and a thought dawned on him as he continued. "Where's Ian? Did you shove him in a closet somewhere to hide him?"

"Nay," Gavin said. "Seems he and Isabo found a way to break the curse."

"He loves my daughter," Angus stated.

"Seems that way," Gavin said as he leaned back in the chair and stretched his legs out in front of him.

"'Bout time that daughter o' mine settled down," Angus stated as he crossed his beefy arms over his chest and settled back to watch the morning news station that Ned had settled on.

A reporter appeared. The scene behind him they recognized. Charred building remains, fire trucks and the police were scattered about behind the pretty young reporter as she gave the sketchy details of the demise of the Gothic bar, Darkest Desires.

"You think he's got to burn every place he goes to the ground," Ned stated point-blank.

"Can not be sure with that one," Angus added. "Just glad that place isn't one o' mine."

Three weeks later...

"You sure about this, Isabo," Ian said as he followed her up the stairs to the bedchamber. "I don't want to be hurting you none."

"Ian," Izzy answered on a husky breath as she stopped on the stair above him, lifted her short belly shirt off over her head and tossed it at him. "I haven't had you inside of me for more days than I care to remember. I'm not waiting any longer."

The sight of Ian's tongue darting across his lips at the sight of her bare breasts made her tingle inside. They hadn't had sex since the night before their battle with the demonic Leod. Ian treated her like a fragile doll and she was tired of it. At first it was cute and endearing how he waited on her hand and foot. But now she was horny and wanted nothing more than to fuck her man.

The stitches were out. The doctor had given her clearance to take things easy. In her book, that meant Ian was fair game.

At the top of the stairs, she wiggled out of her black mini. She knew the moment he caught sight of the beaded thong. His pupils dilated and his nostrils flared, so she added to the tease by twisting her finger in the pearled string and tugging it tight against her clit.

201

"Come on, big boy," she teased in a husky breath, "let's play."

When Ian moved, she squealed, turned and ran into the bedchamber. Together they tumbled onto the bed. Ian managed to take the force of the fall and cradled her from any harm. He flipped her onto her back and lay stationed between her thighs.

"Isabo, I don't want to hurt you, but you're driving me mad with hunger for your sheath."

Izzy spread her legs wide and grinned as she clawed at his kilt, tugging it up to his waist, revealing a solid shaft jutting out from the dark nest of curls below his waist.

"Fuck me, Ian. I need to feel you inside me and I want your cock now."

He didn't need any further request. Ian slid up her body, capturing her mouth as he plunged hilt-deep into the waiting warmth of his love, his *dona leannan*, Isabo.

Also by Tara Nina

ℰↄ

About the Author

ଉ

Tara Nina is a romantic dreamer whose dreams are now a reality through the publication of one of her romantic fantasies. She resides in Northern New Jersey along with her husband, two children, two dogs and a cascade of supportive friends and relatives.

Tara welcomes comments from readers. You can find her website and email address on her author bio page at www.ellorascave.com.

Tell Us What You Think

We appreciate hearing reader opinions about our books. You can email us at Comments@EllorasCave.com.

Why an electronic book?

We live in the Information Age — an exciting time in the history of human civilization, in which technology rules supreme and continues to progress in leaps and bounds every minute of every day. For a multitude of reasons, more and more avid literary fans are opting to purchase e-books instead of paper books. The question from those not yet initiated into the world of electronic reading is simply: *Why?*

1. *Price.* An electronic title at Ellora's Cave Publishing and Cerridwen Press runs anywhere from 40% to 75% less than the cover price of the exact same title in paperback format. Why? Basic mathematics and cost. It is less expensive to publish an e-book (no paper and printing, no warehousing and shipping) than it is to publish a paperback, so the savings are passed along to the consumer.

2. *Space.* Running out of room in your house for your books? That is one worry you will never have with electronic books. For a low one-time cost, you can purchase a handheld device specifically designed for e-reading. Many e-readers have large, convenient screens for viewing. Better yet, hundreds of titles can be stored within your new library — on a single microchip. There are a variety of e-readers from different manufacturers. You can also read e-books on your PC or laptop computer. (Please note that Ellora's Cave does not endorse any specific brands.

You can check our websites at www.ellorascave.com or www.cerridwenpress.com for information we make available to new consumers.)

3. *Mobility.* Because your new e-library consists of only a microchip within a small, easily transportable e-reader, your entire cache of books can be taken with you wherever you go.

4. *Personal Viewing Preferences.* Are the words you are currently reading too small? Too large? Too… ANNOYING? Paperback books cannot be modified according to personal preferences, but e-books can.

5. *Instant Gratification.* Is it the middle of the night and all the bookstores near you are closed? Are you tired of waiting days, sometimes weeks, for bookstores to ship the novels you bought? Ellora's Cave Publishing sells instantaneous downloads twenty-four hours a day, seven days a week, every day of the year. Our webstore is never closed. Our e-book delivery system is 100% automated, meaning your order is filled as soon as you pay for it.

Those are a few of the top reasons why electronic books are replacing paperbacks for many avid readers.

As always, Ellora's Cave and Cerridwen Press welcome your questions and comments. We invite you to email us at Comments@ellorascave.com or write to us directly at Ellora's Cave Publishing Inc., 1056 Home Avenue, Akron, OH 44310-3502.

MAKE EACH·DAY MORE *EXCITING* WITH OUR

ELLORA'S
CAVEMEN
CALENDAR

✝ WWW.ELLORASCAVE.COM ✝

erridwen, the Celtic Goddess of wisdom, was the muse who brought inspiration to storytellers and those in the creative arts. Cerridwen Press encompasses the best and most innovative stories in all genres of today's fiction. Visit our site and discover the newest titles by talented authors who still get inspired - much like the ancient storytellers did, once upon a time.

Cerridwen Press

www.cerridwenpress.com

LaVergne, TN USA
19 November 2009
164706LV00001B/27/P